Love, Duty, Choice

A Journey Through Dreams and Sacrifices

MANOJ JHA

notionpress.com

INDIA · SINGAPORE · MALAYSIA

CONTENTS

PREFACE

Some stories are not just written—they are lived. Love, Duty, Choice is one such tale, inspired by real events, heartfelt emotions, and the silent battles waged between tradition and love.

Growing up, I witnessed the weight of expectations, the sting of unspoken sacrifices, and the quiet spirit of those who dared to choose their own path. This novel is born from those experiences—of love that defied norms, of duty that questioned the heart, and of choices that changed destinies.

Through Manohar, Simran, and Anjali, I relive the dilemmas that many of us face—do we follow our hearts, fulfill our responsibilities, or surrender to fate? I invite you to step into their world, to feel their struggles, and perhaps, to find a reflection of your own journey.

This book is my tribute to those who dared to choose.

ACKNOWLEDGEMENT

I am deeply thankful to my wife, Nutan Jha, whose unwavering support has been my anchor, and to my children, Nikhil Jha and Nikita Jha, who inspire me every day. The title of this book was decided by my children, making it even more special. A special heartfelt gratitude to my elderly parents, who live with us—your presence, wisdom, and silent sacrifices have shaped my understanding of love, duty, and the choices that define us.

This book is not just a story; it is a tribute to family, perseverance, and the power of belief.

Chapter 1

UNFORGETTABLE DATE

The day began like any other day with the activity of morning life thrilling the Manohar household. The aroma of freshly brewed tea mingled with the faint scent of a bouquet that had arrived early—a thoughtful gesture from Neetu for their wedding anniversary.

Manohar sat by the window in their modest rented house in Noida, watching the city wake up. The familiar chaos of auto-rickshaws honking and vendors shouting had become a comforting rhythm over the years. The world outside moved at its usual pace, but his thoughts were far from ordinary.

June 8th.

The date loomed over him, not like a shadow, but as a memory-laden spectre—both comforting and bittersweet. It was the kind of date you couldn't forget, even if you tried. A day that had tied together the threads of his life in ways he could never have imagined.

"Papa, are you staring at nothing again," his daughter's voice jolted him.

His daughter stood at the kitchen door, her hands on her hips, eyebrows arched in a manner that was unmistakably inherited from her mother.

Manohar smiled faintly and raised his cup. "Just thinking."

"About what?" she asked, sliding into the chair opposite him. "Or is it one of those 'untold secrets'?"

He chuckled and shook his head. "You wouldn't understand just yet. Give it some time."

"Time?" she exclaimed, pretending to be shocked. "Papa, you act like you're from another era!"

Before he could reply, Neetu appeared, wiping her hands on the edge of her saree. "Leave your Papa alone," she said, her voice carrying that gentle authority she had mastered over the years. "He's probably figuring out how to make up for forgetting our anniversary."

The girl smiled, running away before Manohar could defend himself. Neetu lingered, her look softening as she studied him.

"You've been quite normal all morning," she said, resting a hand on his shoulder. "Are you alright?"

Manohar nodded, offering her a small smile. "Just old memories," he murmured.

She didn't press further. Neetu had learned long ago that Manohar's silences weren't always meant to be filled. He carried his past like a secret diary, revisiting its pages often but rarely letting others read them.

The morning unfolded in the usual way, with the house gradually coming alive. By the time breakfast was on the table, his son had stumbled out of his room, slow but cheerful, while his daughter was already glued to her phone, laughing over something she had found.

"Look at this!" she exclaimed, turning her phone towards them. The screen displayed a faded wedding photo of Manohar, clad in a traditional dhoti and kurta, his expression a mix of pride and nervousness.

"I think I looked quite dashing," he said, pretending indignation.

"You look like you're terrified," his son shot back, earning a round of laughter from the table.

"Alright, enough about me. Go find some pictures of your mother," Manohar said, pointing at Neetu.

"Oh no," Neetu interjected, wagging her finger. "Today›s about both of us. You don›t get to deflect."

The room erupted into laughter again, but when the noise subsided, his daughter turned thoughtful. "Papa, why did you get married on June 8th? Was it just a random date, or…?"

Manohar paused, his cup halfway to his lips. "It wasn't random," he said softly, his voice carrying a weight that made everyone fall silent.

"Then why?"

"It's a long story," he replied, setting the cup down. "So, where do I begin?"

Neetu interjected to lighten the mood. "Enough questions for now. We have an anniversary to celebrate, and there's a cake waiting to be cut."

The rest of the day passed in a whirl of activity—grocery runs, last-minute decorations, and preparations for the evening. By nightfall, the family was gathered in the living room, the old wedding video playing on their television.

Manohar watched himself on the screen, his younger self looking tentative yet hopeful. The camera was shaky, the footage slightly blurred, but it still managed to capture the essence of that day.

As the scenes unfolded, his mind wandered to another June 8th, years before the wedding. It was the day he left his small-town life behind, chasing a future he could barely imagine. It was the day an envelope changed everything, bringing the promise of a new career. And it was the day he sat in Bonta Park, his heart heavy with choices he didn't want to make, saying a final goodbye to the one person who had believed in him unconditionally.

The video ended, pulling Manohar back to the present. As his family cheered and handed him the knife to cut the cake, he looked around the room.

"Papa, it's a wonderful wedding day you had," his daughter said again, her voice filled with playful insistence. "Now, you can tell me other memories about this date. I'm sure you've got a few!"

His daughter's wide-eyed eagerness made it impossible to brush her off. Manohar leaned back, letting a soft sigh escape. "Alright," he said. "But remember, these aren't just stories–they're pieces of me."

She smiled, pulling her chair closer, ready to listen. And as the room settled into silence, Manohar began to speak, his voice steady, weaving the threads of a story that had shaped not just him, but the life they now shared.

Chapter 2

THE JOURNEY BEGINS

Manohar Kumar would always remember June 8, 1990. It was the day he left the comforting familiarity of Darbhanga, a small but lively town in Bihar, and stepped into an uncertain future. The morning sun felt unusually bright, almost as if it shared the turmoil in his heart. He was excited to meet his school friends again—friends who had left Darbhanga two years ago to pursue their dreams in Delhi. But beneath the excitement, he felt quiet fear.

His friends had already started building their lives, while he was only taking his first steps towards his goals. This wasn't just a trip to revive old memories. It was the start of something much bigger. His parents, who had given everything they could for his education, had placed their hopes on him. As the train clattered towards Delhi, the weight of it all became clear. This journey wasn't just about reaching a new city—it was about proving he deserved to be there.

When Manohar stepped off the train at New Delhi Railway Station, the scorching summer air hit him like a furnace blast. The overbearing heat seemed to rise from the very ground, amplifying the chaos of the city around him. He stood for a moment on the crowded platform, his modest suitcase in one hand and a battered cardboard box filled with books in the other. The station was a living organism—loud, restless, and overwhelming. Coolies rushed about, their voices merging with the metallic screech of trains and the indistinct chatter of countless travellers. The pungent scent of sweat, smoke, and diesel lingered in the air, creating an atmosphere of urgency and fatigue.

"No, thank you," he declined the coolies offering their services, his voice swallowed by the noise. This was his journey to navigate, and he was determined to carry its weight—both literal and metaphorical.

Crossing the footbridge that connected platforms, he paused to glance at the sea of people below. The crowd was a tapestry of humanity: exhausted families lugging luggage, hawkers shouting about their wares, and weary travellers making their way through the chaos. Every individual seemed locked in a private battle for space, time, or survival.

Descending on the Paharganj side of the New Delhi Railway Station, the harshness of the platform gave way to the jumble of Delhi's streets. Here, the city revealed a different face, one marked by narrow lanes teeming with life. The vibrant chaos was both fascinating and daunting. Small hotels with peeling paint sat cheek by jowl with street vendors selling spicy snacks and hawkers advertising bus tickets to far-off towns. The air vibrated with a symphony of honking, shopkeepers shouting prices, and the steady buzz of voices rising and falling.

Manohar's nerves prickled with the reality of being a newcomer in this sprawling metropolis. Delhi was vast and relentless, a city that neither noticed nor cared for him. But beneath the unease, a sparkle of determination burned.

He wasn't here to get lost in the city's anonymity. He had come with a singular purpose: to rise above the limitations of his modest background by preparing for competitive exams that could carve out a better future for himself and his family.

His family had invested more than their savings in him—they had poured their trust and aspirations into his journey. For them, he wasn't just a young man leaving for Delhi; he was a hope bearer, someone who could transcend the constraints of their small-town life.

As Manohar made his way through the streets of Paharganj, his senses absorbed the city's unrelenting energy. He tightened his grip on his belongings, not just to safeguard them but to steady himself against the whirlwind of uncertainty ahead. It was a small gesture of resolve, a silent promise to himself that no matter how intimidating the city seemed, he would find his place in its chaos.

The air was thick with the aromas of Delhi's street life—*samosas* sizzling in hot oil, the sharp tang of pickles wafting from jars on makeshift carts, and the sweet, spicy scent of tea brewing in dented kettles at roadside stalls. The sounds of the city—honking cars, hawkers shouting their wares, and the constant buzz of life—mixed with the smells created an overwhelming sensory assault.

Manohar moved cautiously, his eyes darting between storefronts and street vendors. The sheer scale of the city unnerved him. This wasn't Darbhanga, the quiet town he had known all his life with its slow-moving cycle rickshaws and familiar faces. This was Delhi—loud, bustling, and relentless. Here, everything seemed to be in motion, and everyone appeared to be in a hurry.

He walked slowly, clutching his suitcase, weaving through the chaos. Rickshaws whizzed by, narrowly missing him. Vendors called out to potential customers, their voices loud and persistent. Pedestrians jostled him as they pushed past. He kept going, though, his gaze fixed on the DTC bus stop ahead.

Manohar had heard about Delhi's buses from a friend back home. They were affordable but notoriously unpredictable. For someone like him with limited money, they were his only choice. He reached the bus stop and found a disorganised crowd already gathered. People pushed, elbowed, and jostled to secure their spots, but Manohar stood patiently at the edge, looking out for the bus he needed.

Sweat trickled down his back, the heat pressing down on him like a heavyweight. He adjusted his grip on the cardboard box of books he carried, his mind wandering to what lay ahead.

Manohar wasn't in Delhi for the usual reasons young men came to the city. He wasn't chasing a seat at Delhi University or dreaming of the student life others around him craved. His ambitions were loftier. He dreamed of cracking the prestigious UPSC exams or at least securing a government job through the State Service Commission exams. Those dreams felt vivid yet distant, shining brightly in his mind but blurred by the reality of his current struggle.

❋   ❋   ❋

As he waited, his thoughts drifted to his journey so far. Back in Bihar, a single decision after the 10th board exams determined the future of most science stream students. You either chose mathematics or biology, sealing your fate as an aspiring engineer or doctor. For Manohar, biology was the clear choice. He had scored well in his 10th and 12th exams and secured admission to a prestigious college in Darbhanga. The path ahead seemed straightforward: study hard, crack the medical entrance exam and become a doctor.

He threw himself into his studies, devoting long hours to mastering his subjects. His first attempt at the state medical entrance examination was heartbreakingly close—he missed the cut-off by just three marks. The failure stung, but it didn't break him. Instead, it fuelled his determination. He enrolled in a B.Sc. (Honours) programme, balancing his college workload with a renewed focus on the medical entrance.

Manohar wasn't alone in this competition. His group of five close friends shared the same goal of becoming doctors. Two of them left for Patna to join coaching institutes that promised better results. Manohar, however, stayed behind. His family couldn't afford the cost of coaching, and he couldn't ask them to stretch themselves further. They had already sacrificed so much to support him.

When the results of his second state medical entrance attempt arrived, they brought heartbreak. He had missed the cut-off again, this time by an agonising two marks. The weight of such a narrow failure crushed his spirit. It felt like fate itself had conspired against him, taunting him with how close he had come. There would be no third attempt. With a heavy heart, Manohar made the painful decision to abandon his dream of becoming a doctor and focus on completing his B.Sc. Honours degree instead.

But even this path was riddled with obstacles. Bihar's universities were tarnished by their delays. A course designed to take three years often dragged on for five, stretching the patience of even the most determined students. These delays weren't just frustrating; they were life-altering. They stole precious years, derailed plans, and left students like Manohar deserted in an endless cycle of waiting. The inefficiency of the system was not just an inconvenience—it was a theft of time, ambition, and opportunity.

It was this relentless stagnation that eventually drove Manohar to look beyond Bihar's borders. He realised he couldn't afford to wait any longer. The world wasn't going to pause for him, and he needed to take charge of his future. Delhi, with its sprawling coaching centres and endless opportunities, seemed like the obvious choice.

Manohar wasn't alone in his decision. Every year, countless students from Bihar embark on the same journey, driven by dreams of cracking the prestigious UPSC exams or securing high-ranking government jobs. For these students, Delhi represented hope—a place where ambition could finally take root. Bihar's reputation for producing bureaucrats was a matter of pride, but it also came with harsh realities. For every success story, countless others failed, their dreams crushed under the weight of competition, financial hardship, or the sheer unpredictability of life in the city.

As Manohar packed his bags after his final exam, the decision to leave felt inevitable. Staying meant more delays, more frustration and fewer opportunities. The broken education system of his home state left him with little choice. Yet, even as he prepared to leave, questions haunted him. Why did it have to be this way? Why did students like him have to leave behind their homes, families, and communities, chasing uncertain futures in far-off cities? What if Bihar had a stronger education system and better job opportunities? Couldn't the exodus of talent be stopped?

These thoughts swirled in his mind as he folded his few belongings and closed his suitcase. The road ahead was uncertain, shadowed by the weight of his past failures and the immense pressure to succeed. Delhi offered no guarantees.

At the bus stop, Manohar shifted his weight from one foot to the other, the cardboard box growing heavier in his hands. He glanced at the crowd again, watching as people pushed their way onto an approaching bus. His mind returned to the present. This was just the beginning of his journey. Delhi was intimidating, but it was also a place of opportunity. He adjusted his grip on his belongings and stepped forward, ready to claim his spot on the bus, and perhaps, in the city itself.

When the DTC bus number 110 screeched to a halt, its brakes groaning under the strain, Manohar noticed with surprise that the usual surge of passengers was missing.

He stepped up carefully through the back door, balancing his belongings as the bus gave a slight lurch forward.

"Timarpur," he said to the conductor, handing over a crumpled note.

The conductor, a weary-looking man whose uniform had seen better days, squinted at him. "Where exactly in Timarpur?"

Manohar unfolded a small piece of paper from his pocket. "This address," he said, pointing to the neatly written words.

The conductor glanced at it briefly and nodded. "About an hour's ride," he replied, punching a ticket and handing it over. "I'll let you know when we get there."

Relieved, Manohar found a seat by the window, placing his briefcase securely next to him and clutching the box on his lap. Outside, the city stretched before him—a chaotic symphony of life, sound, and motion.

The wide road ahead was unlike anything he'd seen in Darbhanga. Cars, buses, and bicycles fought for space in a seamless, honking orchestra of urgency. Vendors lined the sidewalks, hawking everything from colourful shawls to steaming plates of *chaat*. The air was thick with a medley of scents—dust, exhaust fumes, and the faint, tempting aroma of frying snacks. Occasionally, an elegant car would glide through the chaos, its polished exterior in stark contrast to the battered rickshaws and hand-pulled carts moving alongside.

Manohar gazed out, his eyes darting between the ever-changing scenes of the city. Each corner revealed something new—markets bursting onto pavements, families strolling leisurely, and children weaving through the crowds. The energy was infectious, and though he tried to settle into his seat, a restless curiosity kept him glancing out every few moments.

"How far is Timarpur?" he asked the conductor, unable to contain his eagerness.

"Still a way to go," the conductor replied without looking up. "I'll tell you when we're close."

Minutes passed, then what felt like hours. The bus jolted over potholes, the passengers swayed, and Manohar asked again, "Are we near Timarpur?"

The conductor finally turned, his patience wearing thin. "It'll take time! Relax, I'll guide you."

Manohar nodded and tried to sit still, but the anticipation worried him. Outside, the chaos of Delhi seemed to intensify. The road grew narrower, and the traffic denser.

At last, the conductor gestured towards him. "Next stop. Get ready."

Manohar's heart quickened as the bus slowed to a halt. He stepped off, gripping his belongings, and found himself on a quieter street, though still buzzing with activity. The air felt marginally cooler, the hum of the city less overwhelming.

Asking for directions from passers-by, he finally arrived at a modest DDA flat where his friends had set up their temporary home. The building, like many in Delhi, had a weathered charm—its walls streaked with monsoon stains, its balconies adorned with drying clothes.

"Manohar, you're here!" his friend exclaimed, throwing the door open.

"Wasn't too hard to find," Manohar replied, though the maze of streets and the sheer enormity of the city had left him slightly disoriented.

Inside, the flat was humble but lively. Two small rooms, a kitchen, and a balcony that overlooked a dusty courtyard that served as the backdrop for the ambitious dreams of the young men living there. The walls were bare except for a few pinned timetables and motivational quotes scribbled on scraps of paper.

His friends welcomed him warmly, their laughter and companionship filling the room. They spoke of Darbhanga, recalling old times, and asked about mutual acquaintances. Manohar felt a sense of belonging amidst the chatter. The cramped space didn't matter. What mattered was the shared drive—a determination to make something of themselves in this sprawling, unforgiving city.

As he sat there, surrounded by familiar faces in an unfamiliar place, Manohar felt a flicker of hope. Delhi might have been overwhelming, but it also offered a chance–a chance to dream, to strive and, perhaps, to succeed.

Manohar couldn't help but notice the sparse setup in the room—a patchwork of mattresses spread across the floor, each with a rolled-up blanket doubling as a pillow. There wasn't a single cot or bed in sight. An unsteady table, burdened with an avalanche of books and papers, stood at the centre of the room, surrounded by mismatched chairs. Some of his friends were already sprawled on the mattresses, either engrossed in their reading or drifting into afternoon naps. The room's austerity was striking, yet it exuded a sense of purpose.

"This is where the magic happens," one of his friends said with a chuckle, catching Manohar's lingering gaze. "Not much to look at, but it gets the job done."

Manohar nodded, attempting to suppress the disbelief written on his face. The walls told their own story—plastered with motivational quotes, dog-eared timetables, and political maps. These weren't just decorations; they were testaments to the lives being shaped within these four walls. This wasn't merely a rented room; it was a sanctuary of discipline, ambition, and shared dreams.

Manohar placed his briefcase on the floor, his lips curving into a smile spattered with resolve. This would be his new home—humble but brimming with possibilities. It wasn't what he had envisioned, but it was a starting point. From this modest DDA flat, he would chart the course of his future.

For the next three months, Manohar adapted to the rhythms of life in Delhi. He shared the flat with three other friends, each carving out their corner in the cramped quarters. The days fell into a routine—early mornings at the library, afternoons immersed in study sessions, and evenings filled with spirited debates on politics and exam strategies. The companionship was invigorating, but the undercurrent of financial strain grew harder to ignore.

One scorching evening, as the oppressive Delhi heat seemed to seep into every crack of the flat, Manohar sat cross-legged on the floor, his books scattered around him. He couldn't concentrate; his thoughts were weighed down by a growing anxiety. The money his parents sent from Darbhanga was dwindling faster than he had anticipated. Rent, food, and study materials had stretched his modest budget to its limits.

"How do you manage your expenses?" Manohar finally asked Prakash over an economical dinner of rice and lentils.

Prakash leaned back against the wall, his expression one of resigned wisdom. "Delhi isn't kind to wallets, my friend. You have to get creative. Some of us take up tutoring jobs in the evenings—it's a decent way to earn without disrupting studies."

Manohar perked up at the suggestion. "Tutoring? That could work. Do you know anyone who needs a tutor?"

Prakash nodded, a knowing smile spreading across his face. "As a matter of fact, I do. There's a family—the

Malhotra—looking for a tutor for their daughter. They live in the nearby colony."

"Why hasn't anyone taken the job?" Manohar asked, his curiosity piqued.

Prakash hesitated for a moment. "Well, let's just say the girl has a reputation. She's not rude, but she's... particular. Demanding, even. A few tutors have quit because they couldn't keep up."

Manohar frowned but didn't look deterred. "Demanding, how?"

Prakash shrugged. "She's sharp and expects the same from whoever teaches her. But you're smart. I think you'll manage."

The idea preoccupied Manohar's thoughts. He needed the money, and a tutoring job seemed like a logical step. "All right," he said decisively. "I'll go for it."

Prakash's smile widened. "Good. I'll call my friend, Shekhar, and set it up. Don't worry–it's just a couple of hours a day. You'll still have plenty of time for your studies."

Manohar felt a glimmer of relief. It wasn't an ideal solution, but it was a step towards easing his financial strain. The next few days passed in a turmoil as he prepared to take up the challenge.

Manohar nodded, masking his apprehension. Little did he know, this small decision—taking up a tutor job—would lead to a series of events that would shape his life in ways he couldn't imagine?

BOUND BY DESTINY

Manohar felt a knot tighten in his stomach as he approached the Malhotra residence for his first day as a tutor. It wasn't the prospect of teaching that unnerved him but the weight of expectation. This wasn't just about earning money; it was about proving to himself—and his family—that he could thrive in Delhi.

When the door opened, Prakash took the lead. "Aunty, this is Manohar from our area," he said with the confidence that Manohar envied. "He's a brilliant student."

Mrs. Malhotra's face softened immediately, her eyes lighting up with a mix of relief and hope. "Please come in," she said, ushering them into the drawing room.

Manohar glanced around. The house was modest but well-kept; it exuded a sense of warmth that reminded him of home. As he sat down, Mrs. Malhotra spoke, her tone earnest. "It's been so hard to find a tutor who can handle Simran. They all leave after a while."

Manohar nodded politely, though her words fuelled his apprehension.

"Simran, come and meet your new tutor," Mrs. Malhotra called out, her voice carrying down the hallway.

Manohar turned his attention towards the doorway, and in that instant, the world around him seemed to pause. Simran stepped in—short in height, yet carrying an aura that made her presence larger than life. There was something inexplicably captivating about her, a quiet magnetism that drew eyes without demanding them. Her long, silky hair fallen over her shoulders, framing a face that held an effortless glow, as if lit from within. But it was her eyes—deep, kohl-lined pools of unspoken emotions—that truly arrested him. They sparkled with curiosity, reflecting both innocence and a wild spirit. She carried herself with an understated grace, her every movement fluid yet unassuming.

"Good evening, Sir," she greeted, her voice steady yet wrapped in a veil of quiet mystery. It wasn't just the words, but the way they lingered in the air, as if carrying a story of their own.

"Good evening, Simran," Manohar replied with a reassuring smile. "Let's begin, shall we?"

Wasting no time, he dived into the lesson, starting with basic questions about her subjects. It became clear within minutes where the gaps lay. Simran struggled with science and maths, her lack of confidence was evident in her hesitant answers. Yet, beneath the surface, Manohar saw potential—a sharp mind eager to grasp new concepts.

"Your fundamentals need some work, but you're capable," he told her, his tone encouraging. "Give me two months and we'll turn this around."

Simran nodded; her expression was a mix of hope and distrust. It was as if she wanted to believe him but wasn't ready to trust him too easily.

Mrs. Malhotra, who had been silently observing from the corner of the room, exhaled audibly. "Thank you, *beta*," she said, her voice tinged with relief. "I've been so worried about her studies."

Manohar smiled politely, unsure how to respond to her gratitude. As she disappeared briefly into another room, he took a moment to gather his thoughts. When she returned, she was holding an envelope.

"This is for you," she said, placing it in his hand. "If there's anything else you need–materials, extra time–just let me know. I only want the best for Simran."

Manohar hesitated as he reached for the envelope Mrs. Malhotra handed him. He wasn't used to receiving payment before completing a month's work–it felt undeserved. But the sincerity in her eyes and the evident trust she was placing in him left him no room to refuse. Grateful yet uneasy, he tucked the money into his pocket.

As he prepared to leave, Mrs. Malhotra's appearance shifted. She stepped closer, her face clouded with concern. "*Beta*, one request," she began, her voice low but firm. "Please come at 4 p.m. every day. My husband comes home after 5:30 p.m., and… well, its best if you're not here when he's around."

Manohar's brow furrowed. "Why is that, Aunty?" he asked, genuinely puzzled.

She hesitated as if choosing her words carefully. "He has… a temper," she admitted delicately. "And when he's had a drink, he can say things that… it's better if you don't hear them. I don't want you to feel uncomfortable or disrespected."

Manohar nodded slowly, understanding the unspoken tension in her words. "I understand, Auntie. I'll make sure I'm here at 4 p.m."

The weight of her words lingered with him as he stepped out of the house. The streets of the colony bustled with life—children chasing each other, vendors shouting their wares, and the sound of daily chores spilling from open windows. Manohar walked briskly, his hand instinctively brushing against the pocket where the envelope rested. The sensation gave him an odd mixture of relief and responsibility.

Once he reached his small, sparsely furnished flat, he closed the door and leaned against it for a moment, exhaling deeply. He made his way to the bed, sat down, and pulled out the envelope. His hands trembled slightly as he unfolded the notes.

"Ten crisp 100-rupee notes," he murmured, running his fingers over the paper. He counted them once, then again, to be sure. "One thousand rupees," he whispered in wonder.

It was more money than he had expected—more than his parents sent him from Darbhanga each month. The realisation filled him with gratitude but also unease. The advance felt like a lifeline, a beacon of hope in the uncertain maze of Delhi life. Yet, it also came with a shadow of doubt.

"What if I fail?" he thought, the question troubling at the edges of his mind. "What if Simran doesn't like my teaching? What if her parents lose patience?"

He shook his head, forcing the thoughts aside. Dwelling on failure wouldn't help. For the first time since his arrival in the city, he felt a faint sense of stability. The money meant he could cover his rent, buy essentials, and perhaps save a little. But it also came with an unspoken condition: he had to succeed at this tuition.

Simran, his first student, was a 15-year-old girl studying in class nine. She was the daughter of a local businessman, and her parents were determined to see her excel in mathematics. Simran, however, was a study in contrasts. She exuded the confidence of a typical Delhi teenager. Her sharp tongue and casual behaviour made it clear she was accustomed to getting her way.

Manohar soon realised that her approach to studies was as relaxed as her attitude towards punctuality. She would show up late to lessons—or sometimes not at all—her excuses ranging from "I was busy with friends" to "I forgot." Manohar, though inwardly frustrated, knew he couldn't afford to lose this job.

Her parents, despite their daughter's casualness, seemed willing to pay well, and Manohar had no choice but to tolerate her whims. It wasn't an ideal situation, but it was a start. As he stared at the money in his hands, his resolve solidified.

He would make this work—whatever it took. Failure wasn't an option, not anymore.

✳ ✳ ✳

At first, their relationship was strictly professional. Manohar maintained a sensible approach, entirely focused on his role as a tutor. For him, this was a means to earn money and secure his survival in the sprawling chaos of Delhi. Simran, on the other hand, was just a student. Her parents were determined to see her succeed in mathematics—a predictable story in his line of work. Yet, the spark of life has a way of creeping into even the most unexciting routines, and as weeks turned into months, the dynamics between them began to shift.

Simran, initially indifferent to Manohar, found herself growing curious about the man who taught her with such quiet confidence. His unassuming attitude, his stories of a simpler life in Darbhanga, and the dreams he carried despite the odds fascinated her. Manohar was unlike the boys she knew, who were loud and flashy in their attempts to impress. He seemed to carry a world within him, a world she wanted to understand.

Their lessons began to stretch longer than they needed to. Simran, under the pretext of clearing her doubts, started steering their conversations towards his personal life. "How did you manage your studies without coaching?" she'd ask, her eyes lighting up with genuine interest. Manohar would answer, oblivious to the fact that she was listening as much to the pulse of his voice as the content of his words.

Soon, her admiration for him began to evolve into something deeper. She started lingering at the door when he arrived, offering him water or tea before they started. Her questions became more probing, her laughter a little too frequent at his dry humour. She'd fix her hair unconsciously when he looked up from her notebook, and her tone grew softer whenever she spoke his name.

Manohar, however, remained resolute or at least tried to. He noticed the changes—the extra warmth in her voice, the way her fingers brushed against his hand when passing her notebook, the glances that lingered a moment too long— but he chose to ignore them. It wasn't appropriate, he told himself. She was just a child, and he was there to guide her academically, nothing more.

Yet, despite his attempts to maintain distance, he couldn't deny the complications simmering beneath the surface. Simran's growing affection was clear, and it began to seep into the cracks of his carefully constructed walls.

One evening, as their lesson drew to a close, Simran broke the flow of equations and formulas with an unexpected question. They were sitting cross-legged on the living room floor, surrounded by books and notebooks, the warm glow of the setting sun spilling through the window.

"Manohar *bhaiya*," she began, her voice hesitant but her eyes steady. "Do you ever feel lonely here in Delhi?"

Manohar froze, the question catching him off guard. He looked at her, searching for the intention behind her words. "Why do you ask?" he replied, his tone cautious.

Simran shrugged, but her expression betrayed her. "I don't know. You always seem so… serious. Like there's a lot on your mind but no one to talk to about it."

Manohar exhaled slowly, unsure of how to respond. Her insight startled him—how had she noticed something he hadn't allowed himself to admit? He forced a small smile. "Life in a big city isn't easy, Simran. But it's what I chose, so I can't complain."

Her gaze didn't waver. "Still, it must be hard. Being away from home, from family."

There was a pause, heavy with unspoken thoughts. Manohar turned back to the notebook, gesturing towards the unfinished problem. "Let's focus on this question for now. You can't afford to fall behind."

Simran's lips curved into a faint smile, but her eyes remained on him a moment longer. "Okay, *bhaiya*," she said softly, although the way she spoke the word carried an unfamiliar weight.

Simran sat with her chin propped on her hand, inattentively tracing patterns on her notebook as the evening light filtered through the curtains. The usual buzz of mathematical equations and explanations seemed distant. Instead, there was an unusual stillness between them, one that felt both fragile and heavy.

She broke the silence, her voice tentative but probing. "You talk about Darbhanga a lot. Do you miss it? And your family?"

Manohar, caught off guard, paused before nodding. "Yes, of course. I do. But I came here for a purpose–to study, to build a future."

Simran tilted her head, her eyes searching his face as if trying to uncover a hidden layer. "You're always so serious. Don't you ever think about... other things? You know, besides studies?"

The question caught him off balance, like a pebble thrown into still water. Manohar glanced at her, trying to read her intentions. Her expression was calm, but her voice carried an unspoken emotion.

"Simran," he said carefully, "you're young. Right now, your focus should be on your studies, on building your own future."

Simran leaned forward slightly, her voice dropping to a near whisper. "But what if I want something more?"

The words hung in the air like a charged storm cloud. Manohar felt the ground shift beneath him, the weight of her gaze pressing down on him. His pulse quickened, not from attraction but from an acute awareness of how dangerous this moment had become.

"Simran," he said, his voice steady but firm, "I think that's enough for today."

He stood abruptly, gathering his books and papers with deliberate precision. Simran didn't protest, but her eyes stayed fixed on him, her unspoken thoughts loud in the quiet room. As he turned to leave, he avoided her gaze, muttering, "I'll see you tomorrow."

❋   ❋   ❋

The walk back to his rented room felt endless, the streets unfamiliar despite being part of his daily routine. Simran's words replayed in his mind, their meaning and intent gnawing at his composure. She was just 15, and he was here as her teacher, not her friend—or anything else. But even as he tried to dismiss the weight of the conversation, he knew something fundamental had shifted.

In the following days, Manohar made a conscious effort to keep his lessons strictly professional. He arrived, taught the assigned topics, and left without indulging in any unnecessary conversations. But Simran wasn't easily deterred. Her gestures grew more deliberate—offering him tea when he arrived, complementing the colour of his shirts and steering conversations towards personal anecdotes she hoped might spark a connection.

For Manohar, it felt like walking a tightrope. He needed the money from her tuition to make ends meet, yet he knew the situation was precarious. One slip could unravel everything.

It all came to a head one humid afternoon when Simran, her cheeks slightly flushed, asked him if he ever thought about going to the movies. "There's a new one at the cinema near Connaught Place," she said casually, though her eyes betrayed her nervousness. "Maybe we could—"

"Simran," Manohar interrupted, his voice calm but resolute, "I need you to understand something." He set down his pen and turned to face her, his expression serious yet kind. "I am your teacher. You are my student. There are boundaries we need to respect,"

Simran blinked, her confidence faltering. "But I thought... I thought you felt the same way," she murmured, her voice trembling.

Manohar inhaled deeply, choosing his words with care. "I care about you, Simran, but not in the way you think. What you're feeling is natural at your age, but it's important to focus on what matters right now—your studies and your dreams. That's why I'm here."

The words hit her like a gust of cold wind. Tears welled in her eyes, and for a moment, it looked as though she might let them fall. But instead, she drew in a shaky breath and turned her gaze away. "Fine," she said quietly, her voice clipped. "I understand."

Manohar left that day feeling a mix of emotions: relief at having addressed the situation, guilt for the hurt he saw in her eyes, and an inexplicable sadness he couldn't quite place.

In the weeks that followed, the lessons grew colder, marked by a distinct distance. Simran no longer lingered after class or asked questions unrelated to the syllabus. The brightness in her demeanour dulled, replaced by an air of quiet resignation.

Manohar told himself he had done the right thing. He had drawn the line that needed to be drawn—for her sake and his. Yet, every time he saw the shadow of hurt in her eyes, he couldn't shake the feeling that something unresolved lingered between them, like a faint echo of words left unsaid.

And though the lessons continued, the warmth they once shared had been replaced by a fragile silence, both of them navigating the unspoken distance with careful steps.

Manohar nodded, feeling the weight of the trust she was placing in him. As he left the Malhotra home that evening, he couldn't shake the feeling that this wasn't just another job. There was something about Simran, her guarded nature, and her untapped potential, that made him want to succeed—not just for himself, but for her too.

Chapter 4

SPARK OF CHANGE

Simran's transformation over the academic year was nothing short of extraordinary. For a year, science had been her adversary—her disinterest and inconsistent effort weighing her down like a heavy anchor. But something had shifted this year, something that even she couldn't quite explain. Under Manohar's patient guidance, she had not only passed her exams but had done so with decent marks—a feat that had seemed almost impossible just months before. For Simran's parents, the results were nothing less than miraculous.

The day the results came in, Mrs. Malhotra could hardly contain her excitement. She held the report card in her hands like a precious treasure, her eyes sparkling with pride. "Simran! You've done it!" she exclaimed, enveloping her daughter in a tight hug. Her voice trembled with joy. Simran smiled, basking in her mother's praise, her heart swelling with a mixture of accomplishment and quiet relief. Even her father, usually reserved and hard to read, cracked a rare smile. He patted her on the back and, in his uncharacteristically warm tone, said, "Good job, *beta*." His eyes lingered on the grades, disbelieving at first as if trying to confirm that his daughter's success was real.

Yet, amidst their joy, both parents knew that the credit didn't entirely belong to Simran. There was someone else who had played a crucial role in her academic turnaround—a quiet, determined tutor from Darbhanga. Manohar's influence was undeniable, and the Malhotra's knew that without him, Simran's achievement would have remained a distant dream.

The very next day, Mrs. Malhotra, unable to hold back her gratitude, insisted on inviting Manohar over. Simran was bubbling with excitement, eager to express her thanks for what she believed was a life-changing contribution. When Manohar arrived, he was treated like a hero returning from battle.

"Manohar ji," Mrs. Malhotra began, ushering him into their spacious living room, "I don't know how to thank you enough. We had nearly given up hope that Simran would ever pass her science subjects. And look at her now! You've done what no one else could."

Mr. Malhotra, ever the man of few words, joined in with a soft but sincere remark. "We are truly grateful, Manohar. I don't know what methods you used, but you've managed to do what two years of expensive tuition couldn't. You're a godsend."

Manohar, seated awkwardly on the edge of the plush sofa, tried to deflect their praise. He wasn't one for grand displays of admiration. "Sir, ma'am," he said, his voice steady but humble, "Simran worked hard, too. I just guided her. The effort was hers."

Simran, standing in the corner, watched the scene unfold with a quiet smile. There was a certain distance between her and Manohar now—an invisible wall that hadn't been there before. Their relationship had changed the moment he had drawn clear boundaries between them. The warmth that had once marked their lessons had now been replaced by an understanding, a polite distance that neither of them fully acknowledged, but both felt. Still, Simran knew deep down that Manohar's influence had been a turning point in her life, academically and otherwise.

Mrs. Malhotra wasn't satisfied with Manohar's modesty. "No, no," she insisted, shaking her head. "You've done more than just guide her. We've seen the change in Simran. She respects you so much, and that's what made the difference. I don't think she's ever admired a teacher the way she admires you."

Manohar shifted uneasily in his seat, his gaze briefly meeting Simran's. She was looking down at the floor, her cheeks flushed with a faint but distinctive colour. He knew that her parents couldn't see the full picture—that the admiration Simran had for him ran deeper than their understanding. But he kept his composure, knowing that his role had always been clear: to teach, not to become the object of her affection.

"You must let us do something for you, Manohar ji," Mr. Malhotra said, reaching into his pocket and pulling out a crisp white envelope. "This is a small token of our appreciation. Please, accept it."

Manohar hesitated, the weight of the gesture making him uncomfortable. The Malhotra's were clearly well-off, and he could tell that this wasn't just a simple thank you—it was a gesture of deep respect and gratitude. But Manohar, ever humble, gently declined.

"Sir, your appreciation is more than enough for me," he replied with a smile. "I don't teach for rewards. I only wish for my students to succeed, and Simran has done just that."

Mrs. Malhotra clasped her hands together, her eyes misting over with emotion. "You're a rare person, Manohar. Truly. But please, at least stay for dinner. We'd love to have you as our guest."

Manohar finally agreed, and that evening, he found himself seated at the Malhotra family dining table, a place of honour. The dinner was lavish, far grander than the modest meals he was used to in his small rented room. The conversation flowed easily, with the Malhotra's constantly praising him for his efforts, while Simran remained quiet in the background, her thoughts unreadable. Her polite smile didn't quite reach her eyes, and Manohar couldn't help but wonder if there was a storm brewing beneath her calm surface.

As the evening wore on, he began to feel a subtle sense of discomfort. The Malhotra's' gratitude, though genuine, seemed to make the air around him heavy. He appreciated their kindness, but he couldn't shake the feeling that he was treading a fine line—especially with Simran, whose feelings for him had always been something more than simple admiration. Though she had controlled them after his gentle rejection, Manohar wasn't sure how long this delicate balance could last.

As the evening came to a close, Mrs. Malhotra's words lingered in the air. "You're not just a tutor to us anymore, Manohar ji," she said warmly, her voice heavy with emotion. "You're a family member."

Manohar offered a polite smile, but the gravity of her statement weighed on him long after he stepped out of their house. The Delhi streets seemed unusually quiet that night, the usual hustle of the city momentarily subdued. His thoughts swirled as he walked away. Yes, he had helped Simran transform academically—there was no denying that. But what he didn't realise was that his connection to this family was far from over. Beneath the surface, unseen emotions ran deep, and he was only beginning to understand their consequences.

Over the next few months, it was impossible to ignore the glaring change in Simran. Gone was the carefree, distracted teenager who used to approach her studies with indifference. In her place stood a focused, determined young woman, especially when it came to science—the very subject that had once seemed an insurmountable challenge. Her parents, naturally, were thrilled by her progress, but deep down, they knew who to thank for this remarkable transformation. The credit, as far as they were concerned, lay squarely with Manohar.

One evening, as they sat sipping tea in their living room, Simran's father, Mr. Malhotra, took a deep breath before making an offer that had been weighing on his mind for some time.

"Manohar ji," he began, his voice sincere but measured, "you've been a true blessing to our family. Simran's progress is nothing short of miraculous, and we owe so much of that to you. But I also know that living in this city can be tough—especially for someone like you, who's come from outside. So, I've been thinking… why don't you move in with us? I've rented out a room on the top floor, and it's spacious and comfortable. You wouldn't have to worry about rent anymore."

Manohar paused, his fingers curling around his cup. The offer caught him off guard. It was kind, yes, but the idea of living in the same house as Simran made him uneasy.

"That's very generous of you, Sir," Manohar said after a long pause, his voice calm but resolute. "I'm managing just fine where I am. I truly appreciate your kindness, but I prefer to live independently."

Mr. Malhotra's expression flickered, a shadow of disappointment crossing his face, though he quickly masked it with a smile. "I understand," he said, nodding. "But please remember the offer is always open. And if you ever need anything—financial help, assistance with anything at all—don't hesitate to ask. You're like family to us now."

Manohar smiled politely, but his resolve remained firm. While the Malhotra's' generosity touched him, he valued his independence too much to accept. He was determined to keep his professional role intact, no matter how tempting the offer seemed.

Meanwhile, Simran had been quietly observing from a distance. The boundaries that Manohar had set were something she took very seriously. Yet, over the months, her feelings for him had deepened. What had started as admiration for his intellect and kindness had transformed into something far more profound–a first love, one that occupied her thoughts day and night.

As she sat in their study sessions, she couldn't help but watch him intently. She noticed the way he would furrow his brow in concentration and the way his voice would soften when explaining difficult concepts. Every little gesture, every moment of attention he gave her, seemed to solidify her growing affection. Her heart ached with feelings she couldn't express, feelings that had only intensified since the day he had gently turned down her advances. But Simran was no longer a naive teenager. She had matured, and her love for him had matured too.

She worked harder than ever, determined to show Manohar that she was more than just a student. She no longer flirted with him or tried to gain his attention. Instead, she threw herself into her studies, not just to impress her parents, but to prove to Manohar that she could be the kind of person he respected—not just as a student, but as someone he could admire on an equal footing.

Manohar, however, remained oblivious to the deepening emotional complexity of their relationship. He noticed her increased dedication, but he attributed it to her determination to succeed in her exams. He assumed that her earlier feelings for him had faded with time, especially as she had stopped displaying any overt signs of affection. Simran had become the model student—focused, serious, and quietly diligent.

As her next exams loomed closer, the tension between her unspoken love and Manohar's unwavering professionalism continued to build. The Malhotra's, still unaware of their daughter's emotional struggle, continued to invite Manohar for tea, dinner, or simply to chat after lessons. Manohar, ever the professional, politely declined each time, maintaining a careful distance, but the lines between tutor and student were becoming increasingly difficult to define.

The unspoken bond between them grew, but so did the quiet tension—both invisible and undeniable. And as Simran prepared for her exams, she knew that this delicate balance couldn't last forever.

The evening passed in a blur of compliments, laughter, and the clinking of silverware, but the unease that lingered in his chest refused to dissipate. For all the warmth and kindness he had received, Manohar knew that things had irrevocably changed. The space between him and Simran had widened, not just by the boundaries of their teacher-student relationship, but by something far more complex— something that neither of them could fully understand nor navigate.

Chapter 5

I LOVE YOU

The room felt unusually heavy that evening, the quiet only broken by the soft rustle of pages as Manohar packed away his books. Simran sat across from him, her eyes trained on him with a look that wasn't quite like any other she had given before. There was something unspoken, something waiting to be said.

"Manohar *bhaiya*," she began softly, using the respectful title she always did, but her tone was different this time—lower, almost hesitant. "I need to tell you something."

Manohar paused, his hands halting mid-air, sensing the change in the air. His eyes met hers, and for the first time in months, the room felt charged. "What is it, Simran?" His voice was steady, but there was a note of concern threading through it.

Simran took a deep breath as if bracing herself for something. Her fingers twitched in her lap, betraying the calm she was trying to maintain. "I... I've been meaning to say this for a long time now," she said, her voice faltering just a little, "I know you've always seen me as your student and I respect that. But the truth is, I've fallen in love with you."

The words hung in the air like a thunderclap, and for a moment, time seemed to stand still. Manohar froze, the confession echoing in his mind. He hadn't expected it—at least, not so openly, not with such rawness. He thought her feelings had faded, that she had long since moved past whatever fleeting attachment she had once felt. But there she was, looking at him, her eyes filled with a mixture of vulnerability and unwavering certainty. And now, there was no turning back.

Manohar swallowed hard, his mind racing. The boundaries he had so carefully set between them, the ones he had worked so hard to preserve, suddenly seemed fragile, ready to shatter. He looked at her, really looked at her—at the girl who had once been his student, now standing before him with the weight of her confession heavy in the room. Her eyes shone with a passion and sincerity that stirred something in him, something he was reluctant to acknowledge.

For a long, painful moment, neither of them spoke. Simran, sitting there with her hands clenched tightly in her lap, her expression open and expectant. Manohar struggled to find the words that could possibly make this right but found nothing that wouldn't hurt her.

"Simran," he finally said, his voice careful but distant, "I'm... thrilled by what you've said, but I don't think I can give you the answer you're hoping for."

The words hit her like a slap, and her expression faltered. The hope she had held onto so fiercely was dimming. "Why?" she whispered, her voice barely audible, laced with pain and disbelief.

Manohar exhaled slowly, his chest tightening. "It's not just about you and me," he began, his words measured, his heart heavy with the weight of his response. "You're an incredible person, Simran. Any man would be lucky to have you in his life. But my family and my community... they have expectations. I'm expected to marry within my caste, within our traditions. It's something that's been ingrained in me, something I can't just ignore."

Simran's face twisted in confusion and then frustration. "Is that all it is? Caste? Tradition? Does that really matter more than how we feel about each other?"

Manohar's frustration mirrored hers as he rubbed the back of his neck, trying to find a way to make her understand. "It's not that simple, Simran. You don't understand the pressure I'm under. My family sacrificed so much to send me to Delhi, to give me an education. They're counting on me to honour their wishes, to follow the path they've laid out for me."

Simran's eyes blazed, and in a moment of raw emotion, she stood up, her small hands clenched into tight fists at her sides. "What about your wishes, Sir?" she asked, her voice trembling, but with a ferocity that surprised even her. "What about what you want? You've always talked about making your way in life, about doing what's right for you. And now you're telling me that you'll just follow whatever your family expects without thinking about what you actually want?"

The silence that followed was thick, almost suffocating. Manohar stood there, caught between two worlds—one that was all he had known, filled with tradition, obligation, and loyalty; and the other, a world that Simran had opened to him, filled with possibility, love, and a freedom he had never dared to imagine. His heart ached, but his mind remained shackled to the expectations of his upbringing, the weight of his family's hopes, and his own deeply ingrained beliefs.

"I'm not asking you to throw away everything for me," Simran said quietly, her voice softening, though there was still an edge of hurt in it. "I just want you to think about it, to think about us. Think about what could be, what we could be." Her words were like a plea, an offering of herself that Manohar could feel deep in his chest.

But despite the pull of his heart, despite the love he could feel stirring within him, he stood there, unable to respond. The answer, in his mind, was already clear. He couldn't have both worlds, not in the way Simran wanted. And that reality was something he wasn't ready to face.

Simran stood there for a moment, looking at him, her chest rising and falling with the weight of unspoken feelings.

Manohar also stood there, looking down at Simran, torn between two worlds. His mind was a whirlwind, thoughts colliding with each other in a chaotic dance. She had laid her heart bare before him, and despite the quiet strength in her voice, the weight of her words was undeniable. She had spoken her truth, and it left him reeling.

"I care about you, Simran," he said softly, his voice thick with emotion, the words somehow feeling too small for the depth of what he was experiencing. "I really do. But I don't think this will work. I don't think I can give you what you want."

His voice trembled at the end of the sentence, and for the first time, Simran saw the cracks in the man who had always seemed so resolute, so firm in his convictions. His face was soft, vulnerable, but still distant as if he had already made peace with the decision that was breaking her heart.

Simran's face shifted, her expression hardening. The blush of her fair skin deepened, not from shyness, but from the anger and hurt that now burned through her. "You're scared," she accused, her voice cutting through the thick silence like a knife. "You're scared to go against your family, to choose for yourself. But I'm not scared, Sir. I love you. And I thought that maybe, just maybe, you'd love me back enough to fight for us."

Her words stung like a whip, and Manohar flinched as though they had physically struck him. Was he scared? He had always prided himself on being rational and pragmatic. But standing before Simran, the girl whose heart he had come to care for, he wasn't sure if rationality had any place in this moment. She was right, in a way. He had always dreamed of carving out his own path—of making choices that were his, of finding his place in the world, free from the suffocating weight of others' expectations.

But this—marriage, love—was different. It wasn't just about him. His family's approval, their traditions, his community's expectations—it was all tied up in this decision. And, as much as he wished it were different, it felt impossible to disregard them. His mind flashed back to his mother's words, echoing in the quiet room: "Marry within your own. The world is complicated enough—don't make it harder for yourself."

"I can't do this, Simran," he said, the words slipping out with an aching sense of finality. His voice trembled, and he felt the knot in his stomach tighten. "I can't let you get hurt by a love that can't go anywhere. We come from different worlds. I belong to mine, and you belong to yours."

Simran stood there, stunned, her heart shattering as she realised that no matter how much she pleaded, no matter how fiercely she loved him, she could never make him cross the line he had drawn in the sand. It wasn't just about love. It was about loyalty to his family, to the traditions he had been raised with. Those walls were impenetrable.

Tears threatened to spill from her eyes, but Simran held them back, forcing herself to stay composed, even if the hurt inside was overwhelming. She turned away from him, her voice barely a whisper, laden with resignation. "I understand," she said softly. The words pierced like a dagger into his chest. "You'll always choose what's easiest for you, Sir. I was just hoping that, for once, you'd choose me."

And with that, she walked out of the room, leaving Manohar standing there, a man caught between his past and the future he could never reach.

As Simran left, a wave of sadness washed over him, and yet, he couldn't shake the nagging thought that maybe she was right—that maybe in his fear of losing his family, he had lost something more important: the chance at a life with her.

✳   ✳   ✳

Simran had always been different from the girls he knew in his small town. She wasn't bound by the rigid constraints of tradition and the rules of caste and family history that governed so much of his life. She was from Delhi—a city that pulsed with ambition, with the belief that anything was possible if you worked for it. People there didn't let old customs hold them back; they forged their own futures. Success was determined by merit, by drive, not by the circumstances of your birth. And Simran, with her independent spirit, fit perfectly into this world.

She had fallen for Manohar, not because he was perfect, but because he was different. He didn't wear his success on his sleeve and didn't flaunt his achievements or wealth. Instead, he had a quiet kind of strength, an honesty that was rare, especially in a city like Delhi. And though his views on tradition frustrated her, she respected them. She admired the way he lived by his principles, even if those principles kept them apart. But now, in the face of his rejection, she couldn't help but feel that all those principles had turned into walls.

She had loved him—loved him—not despite the differences, but because of them. Simran had been willing to fight for them, for the life they could build together. But standing there in the dimly lit room, the pieces of their world had shifted, and she knew that love alone wasn't enough to overcome the centuries of tradition that Manohar felt so bound to.

And yet, as she walked away, something in her stirred. She couldn't give up, not like this. She would find a way to show him that their love was not something to be contained by caste, by family expectations. It was real, and it was hers. And if Manohar couldn't see that now, she'd just have to make him see it later.

She wasn't one to back down. If love was worth fighting for, she would fight.

Chapter 6

THE MANDAL PROTESTS

Manohar's life in Delhi had fallen into a steady rhythm. His days were a blur of books, notes, and silent hours spent inside the cramped study rooms of his rented flat. He had one goal: to crack the UPSC exams. It wasn't just about the prestige of the civil services, but the promise of a future where he could carve out a life of his own, one that wasn't dictated by the narrow confines of his small-town upbringing. His routine was simple and predictable—study, study, and then a trip to Jawahar Book Depot in Jia Sarai for a fresh stack of books.

But in August 1990, something changed. The air in Delhi, thick with heat and dust, seemed to crackle with a new kind of energy. Tension simmered just below the surface, ready to burst.

On August 7, the news broke with the ferocity of a storm. The Prime Minister, V.P. Singh, announced a policy that would change the course of the country. The Other Backward Classes (OBCs) were to receive 27 per cent reservation in Central government services and public sector jobs. It was a move that stemmed from the Mandal Commission's recommendations, a report from 1979 that aimed to address the systemic caste discrimination that had long plagued India. The decision raised the total reserved quota for OBCs, Scheduled Castes, and Scheduled Tribes to 49 per cent.

Manohar sat frozen as he read the announcement in the newspaper. His mind raced; his emotions were conflicted. He had spent his life striving for a fair chance, believing in merit and hard work as the path to success. The idea of reservations, a system where positions in government jobs were set aside for those from specific castes, seemed to him like a challenge to everything he had worked for. It was easy for him to feel that way, but the longer he thought about it, the more he realised how complex the issue was.

At first, he tried to push it aside. His focus had to remain on his studies; the UPSC exam was just months away. But Delhi was not letting him forget. The campus protests began almost immediately. The North Campus, where Manohar spent most of his time, became a hotbed of dissent. Students from every corner of India rallied on the streets, chanting slogans and waving banners demanding the government to reverse its decision. The atmosphere was charged with emotion—outraged voices, raised fists, and the palpable sense that something significant was unfolding.

One evening, after another long study session, Manohar returned to his flat to find the usual calm shattered. Outside the gates, a group of students was shouting, organising protests, and calling for action. As he walked past, one of his friends, Prakash, caught his eye.

"Are you coming to the rally tomorrow?" Prakash asked, his face tense, his voice thick with frustration.

Manohar stopped in his tracks, unsure. "I don't know, Prakash. I understand why everyone's upset, but this policy... it's not as simple as it seems. What if it's a step towards justice for those who've been left behind for so long?"

Prakash's expression darkened. "Manohar, they're turning the system upside down! How can anyone compete fairly when half the seats are reserved? It's not about justice—it's politics, plain and simple. They're messing with our futures."

Manohar didn't have a response. The words felt heavy, but they didn't feel completely right either. His mind was divided, caught between the urgency of his studies and the growing unrest around him. How could he not be swept up in it? The protests were everywhere now—the roads were blocked by angry students, university classes suspended, and even the usually quiet Jawahar Book Depot was caught in the current of political upheaval. The bookstore, which had always been his sanctuary, now buzzed with heated debates, the scent of tea mixing with the air of frustration. The discussions at tea stalls had shifted from preparation strategies for the UPSC to passionate arguments about identity, caste, and the future of the nation.

But it wasn't until September that everything took a terrifying turn.

The country was jolted awake when news spread about Rajeev Goswami, a student from Deshbandhu College, who had set himself on fire in protest against the Mandal Commission's implementation. His self-immolation, broadcast across television screens and splashed across newspapers, shocked the nation. Goswami survived, but his act of desperation became a symbol of the fury that had taken over the student community. In the weeks that followed, more than 200 students attempted self-immolation. Over 60 of them died from their injuries.

Manohar read the reports with growing horror. The protests had escalated far beyond anything he could have imagined. The city, which had once represented opportunity and hope, now felt like a battlefield. The streets outside his flat were filled with angry crowds, their chants echoing through the night. The smell of burning tyres filled the air, mingling with the sharp, acrid scent of fear. Police sirens wailed in the distance, a constant reminder that the situation was spiralling out of control.

Despite the chaos surrounding him, Manohar kept his eyes on his goal. The UPSC exams were still looming large on the horizon, and he couldn't afford to be distracted. But it was impossible to ignore the significance of the moment. The Mandal Commission's decision wasn't just about a policy; it was about the very identity of the nation. It was reshaping the landscape of opportunity, pitting the ideas of merit against the deep-seated inequalities that had long defined the social fabric of India.

Manohar realised that the UPSC exam, which had once seemed like the ultimate test of his abilities, was now part of something much larger. The protests, the self-immolations, the cries for justice—they were no longer distant echoes. They were part of the reality he was living in. Whatever happened in the coming months, the Mandal Protests would leave their mark on the country's future, and his own.

Manohar walked through the narrow lanes of his rented building, his mind weighed down by a storm of thoughts. His usually sharp focus on UPSC had been fractured, lost in the whirlwind of protests, marches, and heated debates about the Mandal Commission. He had always prided himself on his dedication, but the political upheaval around him had started to seep into his thoughts, pulling him away from his books and his goal.

Weeks had passed since the announcement, and with each passing day, the atmosphere around him grew more charged. What started as a distant policy now felt like a battleground for the future of an entire generation. He found himself deeply involved in the student protests, marching alongside his peers, attending rallies, and strategising against the government's decision. It was a cause that felt personal. But at the same time, the relentless energy that the protests demanded had begun to erode his focus. The once-structured study hours were now a distant memory, his notes gathering dust in the corner of his small room.

Even Simran, who had once been the centre of his tutoring sessions, had started to notice the shift. Manohar's absences had become more frequent. His mind was far from the pages of history and public administration; it was consumed by the growing tension around him. Mrs. Malhotra, ever observant, had already made her quiet observations, her concerns lingering in the back of his mind.

One afternoon, after nearly a week of avoiding her house, Manohar decided to visit Simran. As he stepped into the familiar space, he was met with her worried gaze. Simran, always perceptive, handed him a glass of water, her expression reflecting a mix of concern and curiosity.

"Sir, what happened?" she asked gently, her voice filled with worry. "You look exhausted, both physically and mentally."

Manohar sighed heavily, feeling the weight of the past few days pressing down on him. He had grown accustomed to the unrest outside, but at that moment, the reality of it all felt particularly suffocating. "You know, these days, we're caught up in a movement," he said, his voice tinged with frustration. "The government's reservation policy... it's dominating everything."

Simran's brows furrowed, sensing the gravity of the situation. "But why, Sir? What's so troubling about it?" Her question was simple, but it struck at the heart of the matter.

Manohar sank into the chair, the exhaustion of weeks of unrest showing on his face. "It's about the Mandal Commission's recommendations," he began, his tone more serious now. "The government is implementing a 27% reservation for OBCs. For people like me, from the general category, it means a massive reduction in our chances of securing government jobs. It feels like our future is being decided for us, based on something that's not in our control."

Simran, her face thoughtful, leaned in closer. "But, Sir... isn't that the point of reservation? To help those who've been left behind for so long? Doesn't it make sense for them to have a chance now?"

Manohar's frustration began to bubble over, and he leaned forward, his voice rising slightly. "It's not that simple, Simran," he said, his eyes burning with a mix of anger and confusion. "Yes, the reservation was meant to help those who have been oppressed, but now it's been twisted into something else. It's become a political tool, and the system is being rigged. People like me, who've worked hard, now have to compete for fewer opportunities just because of where we come from."

Simran sat back, her expression thoughtful. "But, Sir... don't you think the real problem is the caste system itself? Why should caste matter when we talk about jobs and opportunities?"

Her words, calm yet direct, caught Manohar off guard. He had never really thought about it that way. "No, I don't believe in the caste system," he replied slowly, his voice faltering. "But this policy... it feels unfair. We're not trying to push anyone down. We're just trying to keep our place, the same way we've always worked for it. It's like we're being punished for something we didn't cause."

Simran's brow furrowed, clearly still processing his words. "But, Sir... if you keep opposing the reservation policy, aren't you just perpetuating the same system that has hurt so many for centuries?"

Manohar was taken aback. This wasn't a challenge he had expected from her. Simran, who had always seemed so focused on her own studies, was now questioning his very beliefs. He paused, unsure of how to respond.

"I'm not saying that caste should exist," he said slowly, his thoughts disjointed. "But this reservation policy isn't the solution. It's creating division. Instead of helping us focus on our futures, it's turning us against each other."

Simran nodded, her expression softening as she processed his words. "I see what you're saying, Sir. But I also think that maybe you're too focused on your own situation. There's a bigger picture here, something we can't fully grasp yet."

Manohar didn't answer immediately. Her words echoed in his mind, forcing him to confront something he had never considered: perhaps his frustrations were rooted not just in the policy, but in a deeper, unexamined belief about caste. The realisation made him uncomfortable, but he couldn't ignore it.

As he left the Malhotra house that evening, Manohar couldn't shake the feeling that Simran had seen through him. Her questions, simple yet profound, had revealed something he hadn't fully acknowledged. For the first time, he wondered if his fight was truly about the reservation policy, or if it was about something deeper within himself–a belief in a system he had never questioned before.

In the months that followed, with the stability of regular income from tutoring, Manohar was finally able to refocus on his UPSC preparations. No longer burdened by the stress of financial insecurity, he immersed himself in his studies once more, devouring books and guides that would help him achieve his goal. But even as his evenings were spent surrounded by volumes of material, the quiet hum of Simran's words lingered in the back of his mind, challenging him to confront not just the political climate, but his own deeply held beliefs about caste and equality.

Chapter 7

JAWAHAR BOOK DEPOT

In the heart of South Delhi, tucked away on a quiet street in Jia Sarai, there was a place that had become a sanctuary for students like Manohar—Jawahar Book Depot. It wasn't a typical bookshop; it was a lifeline, a steady source of guidance, and above all, a place that understood the quiet desperation of every aspiring student.

Manohar had first stumbled upon Jawahar Book Depot during his early days in Delhi. The shop's exterior was anything but remarkable. A narrow entrance, with books stacked haphazardly on the pavement, hardly suggested the treasure trove that lay within. Yet, once inside, the world changed. The cramped space, filled with towering shelves, seemed to contain everything one could possibly need for the ambitious journey of cracking competitive exams. History, geography, economics, the pages of these subjects filled the air, each book a potential key to unlocking the future.

Manohar wasn't just there to buy books; he had come to find a sense of belonging. The owner, a man in his early 50s with greying hair and a perpetual smile, knew the dreams of every student who crossed the threshold. He knew exactly which books would help, which ones would speak to the aspirants, and more importantly, which ones would be the most practical for the demanding UPSC exams.

"*Namaste, bhaiya,*" Manohar greeted the owner one afternoon, his voice a mix of exhaustion and hope.

"*Ah, Manohar! Tum phir aaye ho? Kya chahiye aaj?*" The owner's voice was warm and welcoming as if seeing Manohar was the most natural thing in the world. (You're here again? What do you need today?)

"*Bhaiya, kuch nayi books chahiye UPSC ke liye. Is baar history aur geography ka thoda special focus karna hai,*" Manohar replied, the weight of his words reflecting the significance of his request. (I need new books for UPSC. This time, I want to focus more on history and geography.)

The owner smiled knowingly, his eyes twinkling with a mix of experience and empathy. "*Arre, zaroor! Ek kaam karo, Gupta ka guide le lo. Bohot achi book hai history ke liye. Geography ke liye to Sharma ka map-based study guide best rahega. Aur haan, agar Xerox chahiye to bata dena. Bahut mehengi kitab hai yeh.*" The old man didn't just sell books; he understood the reality of a student's life. (Of course! Take Gupta's guide; it's excellent for history. For geography, Sharma's map-based study guide will be the best. And let me know if you need a Xerox copy. These books are quite expensive.)

Manohar, with his limited budget, preferred the Xeroxed versions, the pages just as useful but far more affordable. "*Haan, bhaiya, Xerox thik rahega. Waise ek baat puchhun? Aapko kitna time ho gaya yeh shop chalate hue?*" Manohar asked, his curiosity piqued. (Yes, brother, Xerox will work fine. By the way, how long have you been running this shop?)

The owner chuckled softly, a deep, resonant laugh that seemed to carry decades of wisdom. *"Beta, main toh yeh kaam shuru kiya jab tumhare jaise hi students yahan aane lage. Pata hai, yeh shop UPSC aur IAS aspirants' ke liye ek jagah ban gayi hai. Har saal kai bache aate hain, kitabein kharidte hain, aur phir kaun pass ho gaya, kaun fail, sab sunne ko milta hai."* (Son, I started this work when students like you began coming here. You know, this shop has become a hub for UPSC and IAS aspirants. Every year, many students buy books, and then I hear about who passed and who failed.)

Manohar was intrigued. *"Bhaiya, kitni baar dekha hai ki log yahan pe struggle karte hain, aur kitne safal hote hain?"* he asked, his voice a blend of curiosity and genuine respect.

"Safalta aur asafalta, beta, yeh sab toh mehnat aur kismat ka khel hai. Par ek cheez yaad rakhna: kabhi haar nahi maanni chahiye," the owner replied, his words simple yet profound. (Success and failure, son, it's all a game of hard work and destiny. But remember one thing: never give up.)

Manohar walked away from the shop that day, his arms full of books, each one a promise, each one a step closer to his dreams. But it wasn't just the books that he carried with him; it was the quiet encouragement of a man who had seen the hopes and struggles of countless students and still believed that success wasn't about never failing, but about never giving up.

The shop wasn't just a place to buy study materials; it was a reminder of the shared journey every student in Delhi undertook, a journey of uncertainty, ambition, and the fierce will to succeed. And with every visit, Manohar found himself more determined, more hopeful, not just about the exams, but about the life he was building for himself.

NO 'AUNTY.' JUST 'MA'AM'

For weeks, Manohar and his friends had been enduring the miseries of their current flat—no water, overcrowded hallways, and the ever-present symphony of late-night debates that echoed into the early morning hours. They were fed up. One evening, in a fit of frustration, they decided it was time to find a new place to live. Armed with nothing but their hopes (and an unhealthy amount of optimism), they set out to scour the narrow streets of Delhi, eyes peeled for any "To-Let" sign.

They knocked on door after door, receiving nothing but a parade of "no's" in return. No one seemed interested in renting to a group of young men who were perpetually apologising for their bad luck with flats. After an hour of this, they came across a modest house that seemed promising. The doorbell rang. And they waited.

The door swung open to reveal a woman in her early 40s, though her flawless appearance and sharp features made her look much younger. She carried herself with a confidence that was hard to miss, almost as if her aura could be measured in watts. Her *sari* was perfectly tied, her hair neatly pulled back, and she seemed like the kind of person who, if she had a list of things to do that day, had already ticked off "owning the universe."

"Yes, who do you want to meet?" she asked, her voice brisk but polite as if she were used to being the gatekeeper to something much more important than mere rental inquiries.

Manohar's friend, who had been nudging him forward for the last few minutes, cleared his throat, adjusted his shirt, and said, "Is there a flat for rent here, Ma'am?"

The woman looked them over for a moment, sizing them up. Then, with a nod, she confirmed, "Yes, yes, there is."

Manohar's friend was about to say more when Manohar, in his usual state of overzealousness, interrupted him with a little too much enthusiasm. "Aunty, can we have a look at the flat?"

The words hung in the air, and for a second, the world seemed to freeze. The woman blinked. Her face twitched. And then, just as quickly, she regained her composure, though something in her eyes suggested that Manohar had just made a tiny, unintentional social faux pas.

"You can come tomorrow," she said, her voice now noticeably cooler. "I'll show you the flat then."

The door closed with a soft click.

As the group trudged back to their current, decidedly unsuitable living space, Manohar's friend couldn't contain himself anymore. "Manohar, why did you call her 'aunty'? We'll never get that flat now!"

Manohar, still blissfully unaware, shrugged and gave a clueless grin. "What's wrong with calling her aunty? It's polite, right?"

His friends groaned in unison. "This is Delhi, Manohar! Middle-aged women don't like being called aunty, especially when they go to great lengths to look younger. You—ugh, let's just see what happens tomorrow."

The next morning, they returned, hopeful but a little nervous. The woman answered the door once again. This time, however, she didn't seem to recognise them. Or maybe she just didn't want to.

"Oh, the flat?" she said, her smile polite but distant. "Sorry, boys, I've already given it to someone else."

Manohar's friends shot him a look so sharp it could cut glass. The unspoken message was clear: "I told you so."

Disappointed, flatless, and slightly embarrassed, the group shuffled away from the house. As they walked down the street, Manohar's friend muttered under his breath, "Next time, remember—no aunty, just ma'am or nothing at all."

And just like that, 'auntie' became a running joke in their group. For weeks, it was all they could talk about, making fun of Manohar's seemingly innocent blunder. But beneath the laughter was a slow-burning realisation for Manohar—life in Delhi came with a different set of rules. Unwritten rules. Social codes he was still trying to decode. The city had a way of keeping you on your toes and fitting in required more than just a good education and a sharp mind. It required finesse, and, apparently, a more careful use of titles.

Chapter 9

GROWING AFFECTION

Simran had always been clever—quick-witted, sharp, and effortlessly charming—but now, something different was stirring within her. She wasn't just interested in doing well in her studies or impressing Manohar with her academic prowess. No, she had a more subtle, more personal goal in mind. She wanted to break down the emotional barriers he had so carefully constructed around himself. She wanted him to see beyond the student-teacher relationship, beyond the textbooks—to the person she was becoming. And so, she started with the small things—the little, everyday gestures that seemed insignificant but carried so much weight.

During their tutoring sessions, she no longer just focused on solving problems or finishing exercises. She began asking him, again, about his life in Darbhanga, his family, and the dreams that kept him awake at night. She wanted him to know that she cared—about him, about his story, about his struggles. It wasn't just academic success she was after—it was a connection, a deeper understanding of the person he was. After all, love wasn't built on formulas and equations but on moments of vulnerability and shared truths.

As they spoke, she listened—really listened—absorbing every word he said, each one revealing a little more of the man behind the tough exterior. She admired his devotion to his family, his quiet strength, and his unwavering commitment to his roots. Yet, it hurt her. She knew that it was his commitment to those very roots that was keeping them apart. And still, she hoped that by showing him a different side of herself, a side that was thoughtful, mature, and willing to understand his world, he might begin to see her not as just another girl from Delhi, but as someone who could fit into his life. Someone who could be more than a fleeting moment.

Simran's efforts didn't stop at her words. She knew that to truly understand him, she had to understand his world—the culture, the traditions, the values that shaped him. So, she started asking questions, subtle ones—about his family's customs, about his beliefs, about the foods he loved. She wanted him to know that she respected his roots, even if she didn't always agree with the constraints they placed on him. She didn't believe in the caste system, but she was willing to look past it. Love, she knew, was about compromise. And if it meant bridging the gap between their worlds, she was ready.

At home, Simran's parents were completely unaware of the emotional struggle that was playing out between the two of them. They only saw the surface—Manohar was a hardworking, well-mannered young man, and they liked having him around. He was a regular at their dinner table, the kind of guest who brought a sense of warmth and respect. And each time, Simran found herself stealing glances at him, hoping that this time, maybe, he'd see her as something more than just his student. More than just a familiar face across the dinner table.

But despite all her efforts, Manohar remained distant. He respected her more than ever—his admiration for her intellect and her newfound maturity was evident. She was no longer the carefree Delhi girl who once laughed off her mistakes or flitted through life without a care. Now, she was someone who took her education seriously, someone who was thoughtful, capable, and determined. Yet, despite this transformation, the invisible wall between them was still there. And as much as she tried to bridge that gap, it seemed as though he was unwilling to let her in.

Simran knew, deep down, that simply having more dinners or engaging in casual conversation wouldn't be enough to win him over. She had to show him that she understood his fears; but more importantly, she had to prove that love was stronger than those fears. She believed that if she could get him to see beyond the boundaries of caste and tradition, he would realise that their connection— what they shared—was worth fighting for. But how? That question kept her up at night. She didn't want to pressure him, didn't want to force him into a decision he wasn't ready for. But she also couldn't just let him slip away. Her feelings for him were real, and she was determined to show him that.

So she kept at it—quietly, patiently. Every tutoring session was another opportunity to show him who she was, what she stood for, and what she wanted. She resolved to keep being the best version of herself, hoping that, in time, he would see that love was not about traditions or expectations. It was about two people who saw each other for who they truly were and chose to stand by one another, no matter the obstacles. And, just maybe, one day, Manohar would choose her.

Meanwhile, Simran had another way to impress him: her academics. She knew that if she could excel in her studies and meet his expectations in the exams, he would see that she was serious—not just about her education, but about him too. So gone were the days when she'd let her mind wander, distracted by daydreams or social events. She approached every lesson with laser-like focus, determined to master every subject, every concept, and every formula. She pored over her textbooks with a level of carefulness she hadn't known she was capable of, especially in the subjects she had once struggled with. Studying had stopped being a chore; it had become her mission.

Manohar noticed the change immediately. During their tutoring sessions, Simran was no longer the playful girl who'd let her mistakes slide or get frustrated when things didn't come easily. Now, she was confident, sharp, and always prepared. Every time he asked her a question—whether it was a tricky science problem or a philosophical debate—Simran answered with precision, her understanding deeper than ever before.

At first, Manohar was pleased with her progress. He had always believed in her potential, and now, seeing her finally take her studies seriously, he felt a swell of pride. But over time, something else began to nag at him. He understood that this transformation wasn't just about academics. There was something else behind it. Something deeper. Simran's quiet determination—it wasn't just about studying. It was about him. She wasn't just trying to impress him; she was trying to break through to him. And with every passing day, he found himself noticing her more—not just as a student, but as someone who might just be capable of changing everything he thought he knew about love.

"Simran," Manohar said one evening, his voice thoughtful, as he leaned back in his chair, looking at her with a rare sincerity. "I'm really impressed with how far you've come. You've been working incredibly hard and it shows."

Simran's heart skipped a beat. It was the moment she had been waiting for, the moment when all her efforts, all the hours she had spent poring over textbooks, would finally be acknowledged. His words, simple as they were, felt like a precious gift. She gave him a small, modest smile, doing her best to keep her emotions in check. "Thank you, Sir. It's because of your teaching. You've helped me a lot."

Manohar shook his head, a modest gesture that always accompanied his compliments. "No, Simran. You're the one putting in the hard work. I'm just here to guide you."

For Simran, hearing this was like a weight lifting off her shoulders. His approval was everything. It wasn't just that she wanted to impress him–it was that she was genuinely growing, learning, evolving. She wasn't just working for the grades anymore; she was working for herself. And somehow, that made the effort feel even more worthwhile.

As Simran's progress became more evident, Manohar couldn't help but feel a quiet sense of pride. He had always believed in her potential, but now he saw it unfolding before his eyes. It wasn't just about teaching her the formulas or solving equations–it was about witnessing her transformation and seeing the strength of her character bloom through her dedication. His role as her tutor had taken on a new meaning.

And as much as Simran was changing, so was Manohar. Their tutoring sessions, which had once been purely academic, now carried a deeper, more personal connection. They exchanged ideas with ease and talked about more than just the syllabus. He began to enjoy their conversations, the back-and-forth that allowed him to see Simran not just as a student, but as an individual with her own thoughts, dreams, and convictions.

One evening, after Simran had breezed through a particularly challenging set of questions, Manohar couldn't hide his admiration. He leaned back in his chair, watching her with a look of genuine respect. "You've really come a long way, Simran," he said, his voice filled with warmth. "I think you're more than ready for your exams. You've worked harder than anyone I know."

Simran's face lit up. Her heart swelled with pride, and for a moment, she felt as if the world had come to a standstill. This was it. This was why she had pushed herself so hard. Not just to pass her exams, but to earn his respect, and his approval. She had always known, deep down, that actions spoke louder than words. If she worked hard enough, if she showed him how serious she was about her future, he would see her—not just as a student, but as someone worthy of his admiration.

"Thank you, Sir," she said in a soft voice, her eyes meeting his with a quiet sincerity. "I just want to make you proud."

Manohar smiled at her, but there was something behind that smile–a shadow of hesitation that Simran couldn't quite place. He was proud of her, of course. He saw how far she had come, how much she had grown. But there was a deeper layer to his emotions, a quiet unease that lingered beneath the surface. He wasn't just proud of her academic progress; he was proud of her as a person–of the way she had transformed before his eyes.

But Simran was unaware of that lingering weight. For her, the moment was perfect. She had done it—she had impressed him. She had worked hard and earned his respect. It wasn't enough for him to just see her as a diligent student. She needed him to see her as someone capable of standing by his side, as someone who could be more than a pupil, someone worthy of his affection.

In the quiet spaces between their words, Simran knew that academic success alone wouldn't win Manohar's heart. But for now, it was enough. She had made him proud, and that pride, she hoped, would pave the way for something more. Every compliment, every nod of approval, felt like another plank in the bridge that she was trying to build between them. Slowly but surely, she was breaking through. And as long as she kept working hard, kept striving for excellence, she believed that one day, he would see her not just as his student, but as someone who could stand beside him—someone worthy of a place in his life.

As she looked at him, watching the thoughtful expression on his face, Simran knew this was just the beginning. It wasn't about passing exams. It wasn't even about winning his heart. It was about showing him, in every way she could, that she was more than what he might have imagined. That one day, he would see her for who she truly was—someone who could be his equal.

Chapter 10

SIMRAN & ANJALI

Simran's transformation was the talk of the school. Murmurs about her brilliant rise from an average student to one of the brightest in her class echoed through the corridors. During lunch breaks, when most conversations revolved around weekend escapades or the latest crushes, her academic brilliance became an unexpected centrepiece. Her closest friends, though happy for her, couldn't help but feel a tinge of curiosity— or was it envy?

It wasn't long before Anjali, her childhood bosom friend, decided to get to the bottom of the mystery. One sunny afternoon, as they sat in the busy school cafeteria, surrounded by trays of half-eaten sandwiches and clinking glasses of lemonade, Anjali couldn't hold back anymore. She leaned forward, her tone as casual as she could muster.

"Simran," she began, her voice laced with curiosity, "what's going on with you? Seriously, it's like you've had a complete makeover—academic edition. You're practically excelling in every class test."

We're all dying to know... what's your secret?"

Simran paused, mid-sip, and glanced at Anjali. A faint smile crept across her lips as she placed her glass down. She knew this moment would come. How could she hide it from Anjali, her best friend, the one person who had seen her through every joy and heartbreak since kindergarten?

"It's... well," Simran hesitated, her voice barely above a whisper, "it's because of Manohar Sir. He's the one who's pushed me to do better."

Anjali's eyes sparkled with intrigue. "Manohar Sir? That new tutor you mentioned? What's so special about him?"

Simran's cheeks turned a soft shade of pink as she toyed with the edge of her napkin. "He's not like other teachers," she said, her words deliberate. "He's honest, driven, and... different. He doesn't just teach from books; he makes you think. I guess I wanted to prove to him—and maybe to myself—that I could be more than just average."

Anjali tilted her head, studying her friend. The hesitation in Simran's voice, the soft blush on her cheeks—it was all starting to add up. "Simran," Anjali asked, lowering her voice conspiratorially, "do you... like him? I mean, more than just as a teacher?"

Simran froze. Her heart seemed to skip a beat, and for a moment, she wished the ground would swallow her whole. But this was Anjali—her Anjali. There was no point in pretending. With a deep breath, Simran looked down at her hands and said softly, "Yes, I do. But it's not that simple."

Anjali leaned closer, her expression shifting from curiosity to concern. "Why not? If you love him, why not tell him how you feel?"

Simran sighed, the weight of her emotions pressing heavily on her chest. "He's very traditional," she explained. "He doesn't believe in relationships outside his caste. He's made that clear. No matter how much I try, I can't change his mind."

Anjali frowned, her fingers drumming thoughtfully on the table. "That's tough," she admitted. "But you've always been stubborn about what you want. If anyone can change his mind, it's you."

Simran shook her head, a faint smile playing on her lips. "I've tried, Anjali. I really have. I've worked so hard, hoping he'd notice, but it's like there's this wall I can't break through."

A mischievous glimmer appeared in Anjali's eyes. "Alright, then," she declared. "If you can't change his mind alone, maybe we need a new strategy."

Simran looked puzzled. "What do you mean?"

"I mean, let's widen his world a bit," Anjali said with a grin. "Let him meet other people and see life from a different perspective. For starters, I could use some tutoring help myself. Maybe if he gets to know me, he'll start to rethink some of his ideas."

Simran hesitated. "I don't know, Anjali. He's very busy, and I don't want to make things awkward."

"Come on, Simran," Anjali urged. "It's worth a shot. Besides, I do need help, and I'll pay him well. It's just a few sessions—three times a week, at most."

After a long pause, Simran nodded reluctantly. "All right. I'll ask him, but no promises."

Simran smiled, a flicker of hope lighting up her heart. Maybe, just maybe, this could be the beginning of a change.

❋ ❋ ❋

Later that evening, as their session drew to a close, Simran mustered the courage to broach the subject. With her heart pounding, she looked up at Manohar as he packed his books.

"Sir," she began hesitantly, "I have a small favour to ask."

Manohar looked up, his expression calm and encouraging. "What is it, Simran?"

"My friend Anjali needs some help with her studies," Simran explained. "She's willing to pay for a few tutoring sessions—just three times a week. I told her I'd ask if you'd be interested."

Manohar studied her face, his brows furrowing slightly. Simran held her breath, hoping against hope that he'd agree.

Manohar sat back in his chair, a slight frown crossing his face as he considered Simran's request. "I'm already quite busy, Simran. With my studies and your sessions, I'm not sure if I can devote time to another student."

Simran felt a rush of disappointment wash over her, but she quickly masked it with a soft, pleading smile. "I understand, Sir. But it's just for a few months. Anjali needs help and you're the best teacher I know. I'm sure she'll benefit from your guidance."

Manohar sighed, rubbing his temple as he thought it through. The extra money would help with his living expenses, and he had always prided himself on being a dedicated tutor. But his days were packed. Between his studies, preparing for exams, and tutoring Simran, he had barely any time left to breathe.

Still, there was something in Simran's tone that tugged at him. He had always admired her sincerity and hard work. She had come so far in her studies, and he knew how much it meant to her to see her friends succeed as well. Perhaps, if this was something that mattered to her, it was worth squeezing into his already tight schedule.

"All right," he said finally, giving in with a reluctant nod. "I'll do it. But only for a few months. I can't commit beyond that."

Simran's face lit up with a wide grin, her eyes shining with relief and gratitude. "Thank you, Sir! Anjali will be so happy!"

Manohar gave a small nod, but as he packed his books into his bag, a question lingered in his mind. Why had Simran been so insistent on this? He had heard Anjali's name before, of course, but it seemed odd that she would go to such lengths for a friend's tutoring. It wasn't like Simran to push so hard for something that wasn't directly related to her progress.

He brushed the thought aside, though. He was a tutor, and helping students was his job. Besides, it was only for a few months. What difference could it make?

SECOND TUITION

Manohar stepped off the DTC bus, the cool evening breeze brushing against his face as he walked towards Anjali's apartment complex. The towering buildings that loomed before him seemed almost foreign, their windows twinkling with lights like stars in a concrete sky. They stood in sharp contrast to the more modest surroundings he was used to. As he neared the entrance, a uniformed security guard stopped him, eyes scanning him with sharp suspicion.

"Who are you here to meet?" the guard asked, his tone cautious. "What's your purpose? Do you have an appointment?"

Manohar, taken aback by the barrage of questions, gathered his composure and replied politely, "I'm here to tutor Anjali. Her father, Mr. M. Saxena, has asked me to come."

The guard raised an eyebrow, his gaze lingering on Manohar a moment longer before he picked up the phone and dialled Anjali's apartment. After a few tense moments, during which Manohar shifted his weight from one foot to the other, the guard finally nodded, satisfied with the confirmation he received. With a slow mechanical motion, the heavy iron gates creaked open and Manohar stepped inside.

What he saw next made his heart skip a beat. The vast complex was like something out of a dream—a world of its own. Wide, well-maintained pathways stretched out before him, lined with trimmed gardens that seemed to go on forever. The air was filled with the scent of fresh flowers: dahlias in vibrant hues, delicate roses climbing trellises, and the heady perfume of white lilies. Elegant fountains, their water sparkling in the dimming light, murmured softly in the background, adding to the sense of tranquillity. Imported cars—sleek, polished, and immaculate—sat gleaming under the streetlights, their shiny exteriors reflecting the evening sky.

As he walked further, he noticed couples wandering along the pathways, their casual elegance undeniable. The men wore sharp suits, while the women glided by in flowing dresses, their hair perfectly styled, carrying an effortless air of sophistication. They spoke in soft tones, their gestures graceful. It was a world Manohar had only ever observed from a distance. He suddenly felt out of place, his simple clothes making him acutely aware of the divide between the life he knew and this world of luxury.

When he reached the building that housed Anjali's apartment, a servant opened the door with a neutral expression, asking for his name and instructing him to wait in the hall. Manohar stepped inside; the cold air-conditioned room was a stark contrast to the warmth of the evening outside. The hall was impressive—polished marble floors gleamed under the soft lighting and sleek modern furniture in deep shades of maroon and mushroom created an atmosphere of understated luxury. Abstract paintings adorned the walls, and vases holding fresh flowers sat on carefully placed pedestals. Manohar couldn't help but glance around, taking it all in, feeling like a visitor in a world that wasn't his own.

After a few moments, Anjali's father, Mr. Saxena, appeared. He was a tall man with greying hair, dressed in a casual yet expensive outfit that spoke volumes about his wealth and status. His presence exuded authority, but he greeted Manohar with the polite reserve that often came from those who inhabited a different social sphere.

"So, you're Manohar," he said, offering his hand. "Anjali's told me about you. She says you're a good tutor."

Manohar shook his hand, his grip firm but respectful. "Yes, Sir. I've been teaching your daughter's friend, Simran."

Anjali's father gestured to a nearby seat, and they engaged in a brief conversation. Manohar explained how he had come to Delhi for his studies and was tutoring to make ends meet. The man listened attentively, nodding occasionally, but his tone remained formal, almost distant.

"Well, I appreciate you coming here," he said, after a moment's pause. "Anjali's been struggling in one of her subjects. I'm sure you can help her."

He called out to one of the servants, who swiftly went to fetch Anjali.

When Anjali finally appeared, Manohar was momentarily taken aback. She walked into the room with an air of ease, dressed in denim shorts and a half T-shirt that cleaved to her figure. Her outfit was casual, modern and nothing like what he had imagined a student would wear for a tutoring session. For a moment, he felt a jolt of surprise, his conservative upbringing clashing with the boldness of her appearance.

Anjali, however, seemed completely at ease. She flashed a confident smile and greeted him warmly. "Hi, Sir. Nice to meet you," she said, her voice friendly, her posture relaxed.

Manohar, still recovering from his initial shock, quickly composed himself. He reminded himself that he was here to do a job–to teach, not to judge. The extra money would certainly help, and he was determined to focus on his purpose.

After a brief exchange of pleasantries, Anjali's father spoke again. "I'd like you to come three times a week in the evenings," he said. "Anjali's exams are coming up, and I want her fully prepared."

Manohar nodded, his professional manner returning. "Of course, Sir. I'll do my best to help her."

Her father offered a brief smile, then excused himself, leaving the two of them alone in the room. The silence that followed was broken only by the soft ticking of an ornate clock on the wall, its rhythmic sound almost soothing. Anjali gestured for Manohar to sit at the dining table, where her textbooks were neatly spread out like an artist's palette, full of potential.

"Don't mind my father," she said casually, sinking into the chair across from him. "He's just worried about my grades."

Manohar nodded, still taking in his surroundings. The apartment, with its polished surfaces and polished people, felt far removed from the modest homes he was used to. The servants, the luxury, and the effortless ease with which Anjali moved through the space—it was a world he wasn't quite sure he belonged to.

But he quickly reminded himself: this was a job. And he needed the money. The extra income would go a long way. He could put up with the discomfort for now, he told himself, focusing on what brought him here: tutoring.

As the session began, Manohar pushed aside the distractions, determined to give Anjali the best tutoring he could. He focused on the biology notes spread before them, diving into the complex world of human anatomy with all the seriousness of a seasoned teacher. But still, beneath the surface, something worried him—an unease he couldn't shake. There was something about this new world he was stepping into, this polished life that felt foreign. Anjali's carefree attitude, her confidence—it all seemed so different from the simplicity he had always known. Yet, he pushed those thoughts aside, convincing himself this was just another job, another way to make ends meet.

✳ ✳ ✳

Later that evening, when Manohar returned to his small rented room, he found himself recounting his experience to his friends. They sat around a simple wooden table, the glow from a single lightbulb casting long shadows across the room. His friends listened, wide-eyed, as he described the grandeur of Anjali's place—the sprawling gardens, the sleek cars and the luxury that seemed to emanate from every corner. They were intrigued, especially when he mentioned Anjali's appearance and the confident air she carried.

"You're one lucky guy, Manohar," one of his friends said with a grin. "A rich, smart girl asking you to tutor her in a place like that? And did you say she was wearing shorts? Man, that's a different world."

Another friend chuckled, nudging him playfully. "First Simran, now Anjali. Looks like you've got your pick of Delhi's finest!"

Manohar chuckled along, but deep down, the comparison made him uncomfortable. Yes, Anjali had wealth, she had sophistication, and her lifestyle was a world away from the one he had known. But as he lay in bed later that night, his mind wandered back to Simran.

In the quiet of his room, he found himself comparing the two girls. Anjali, with her modern, sophisticated lifestyle, represented everything that seemed alien to him. Her home was filled with luxury, and she didn't appear to be constrained by the traditions that had always shaped his world. Simran, on the other hand, despite growing up in the whirlwind of Delhi's fast-paced life, seemed to be grounded in a way that Anjali wasn't. Simran had a sincerity about her that Anjali's polished exterior couldn't quite replicate. She didn't flaunt her wealth or her beauty; instead, she carried herself with a quiet resilience, facing her challenges with a quiet determination that was both inspiring and humbling.

Manohar realised, in that quiet moment, that it was Simran's simplicity that drew him in. Her desire to excel academically wasn't about impressing anyone; it came from a place of deep ambition to prove herself to the world, not just to him. In contrast, Anjali's drive, while undoubtedly present, felt more about maintaining an image, about fulfilling an expectation rather than following an authentic passion.

The next evening, as Manohar prepared for his second session with Anjali, he found himself taking extra care. He ironed his shirt with more attention, combed his hair with extra care, and left his room a little earlier than usual. It wasn't about impressing Anjali, he told himself; it was about maintaining a professional appearance. Stepping into her world meant presenting himself with the same confidence she seemed to carry so effortlessly.

When he reached the complex again, the servant recognised him and let him in without hesitation. This time, there were fewer questions at the gate by security guard, and Manohar felt a little more at ease as he made his way back into Anjali's apartment.

Inside, Anjali was already waiting. The books were neatly arranged, and she greeted him with a polite smile, her outfit today more subdued than the previous evening, still stylish but less attention-grabbing.

"Good evening, Sir," she said, offering him a seat. "I've been thinking about the subject I really need help with. It's biology—especially the human anatomy part. I'm struggling to grasp some of the concepts."

Manohar nodded, ready to dive into the lesson, but the quiet voice in his mind kept asking: What world was he truly stepping into?

As he made his way out of the apartment, the weight of the evening's events lingered in his mind. What remained to be seen, however, was how this new tutoring arrangement would affect not only Anjali's grades but also his relationship with Simran—and perhaps even challenge the rigid boundaries he had set for himself.

✳   ✳   ✳

Manohar's tutoring sessions with Anjali had become a familiar routine. Each evening, he'd enter her luxurious apartment, the servant would greet him with a nod, and they'd dive into the lessons. Anjali, with her quick wit and sharp intellect, made the sessions feel less like work and more like an exchange of ideas. Her enthusiasm to learn was contagious, and Manohar found himself enjoying the challenge of breaking down complex concepts for her. It was rewarding in its way, and he was beginning to look forward to these sessions.

But despite his growing respect for Anjali's intelligence and her eagerness to learn, his thoughts couldn't help but return to Simran. Every time he taught her, he was reminded of her quiet determination and genuine sincerity.

Simran's dedication to her studies had never been for show. It came from a deeper place—a desire to prove herself, not just to the world, but to herself as well. She didn't flaunt her achievements or seek validation from others, and that quiet strength drew him in like nothing else.

One evening, as Manohar arrived for yet another session with Anjali, he was more focused than ever. The previous night, he had spent hours reviewing the material, determined to give Anjali the best possible help. When he walked into the apartment this time, he was met with the usual warmth from Anjali, who was already seated at the dining table, textbooks laid out in front of her.

"Good evening, Sir," she greeted him with a casual smile, her tone light. "I've been thinking a lot about our last session, and I think I finally understand the basics. But I still need some help with human anatomy—specifically, the circulatory system."

Manohar smiled, flipping open the textbook. "Don't worry, Anjali. We'll take it step by step. You're doing great so far."

As the evening passed, he couldn't help but notice how quickly Anjali grasped the concepts. She asked questions, took notes, and engaged with the material like a true student. It wasn't hard to see that, with the right guidance, she could excel in her studies. But even as they worked through the material, Manohar couldn't shake the growing unease that had started to form in the back of his mind. It wasn't about the lessons–they were going well–it was about the space he was in, the world that Anjali inhabited.

✻   ✻   ✻

Later, as Simran began to notice the growing connection between Anjali and Manohar, something shifted inside her. At first, she had been happy for Anjali, thrilled that her best friend was receiving the same tutoring that had helped her so much. But soon, she couldn't ignore the way Anjali's eyes lit up when she spoke about Manohar. It was a look Simran recognised all too well, and it filled her with an unease she couldn't explain.

One day, as the two girls stood in the hallway after class, Anjali casually remarked, "You know, Simran, your sir is really something else. He's not just smart—he's handsome too! I mean, every time he speaks, I can't help but admire him more and more. He just has this... confidence."

Simran forced a smile, trying to brush it off. "Yes, he's a great teacher. He helped me a lot last year, too."

But Anjali wasn't finished. "And the way he carries himself? It makes me bold. It's like I can't help but admire him more every time we talk. Don't you think he's... well, kind of irresistible?"

Simran's stomach twisted at the words. She knew Anjali was being playful, but something about the way she spoke about Manohar made Simran's chest tighten. She tried to reassure herself that Anjali was just being friendly—nothing more—but the nagging feeling in her gut wouldn't go away.

The unease followed her into her next tutoring session with Manohar. As they worked through the lessons, Simran's mind kept drifting back to Anjali's words. She was distracted, and it was obvious to Manohar.

"Simran, are you okay?" he asked, pausing as she stared blankly at her textbook. "You seem a little off today."

Simran quickly shook her head, trying to push her thoughts away. "I'm fine, Sir. Just... a lot on my mind."

He studied her for a moment, clearly concerned. "If something's bothering you, you can talk to me about it. I know it's not just about studies."

For a split second, Simran considered telling him everything—the growing tension between her and Anjali, her fears that she was losing him to her friend. But something held her back. What if she sounded petty and insecure? What if Manohar didn't feel the same way? Instead, she smiled weakly and said, "No, Sir. I'm fine. Let's just focus on the lesson."

But as the evening wore on, the knot in her stomach only tightened. She couldn't stop thinking about Anjali's words, the way she'd spoken about Manohar. It was clear that Anjali had a deeper admiration for him than she had let on. And Simran's sixth sense told her that this admiration might not be as harmless as it seemed.

As the lesson ended and Manohar gathered his things, Simran found herself stealing glances at him, wondering if he had noticed the shift in Anjali's behaviour. But he was as calm and composed as ever. To him, everything seemed normal.

But to Simran, things were far from normal. There was a storm brewing in her heart, and she wasn't sure how much longer she could keep it contained.

Chapter 12

SEDUCTIVE TRAP

The afternoon sun was fading, casting long shadows over the street as Manohar approached Anjali's house. He'd been looking forward to their usual tutor session, but today, his mind felt unusually distracted. He flipped through the pages of the lesson plan for the day: the reproductive system. A topic that, despite being entirely academic, always made him feel slightly awkward.

As his finger hovered over the doorbell, the shrill ring echoed through the quiet neighbourhood, causing him to freeze momentarily. Normally, Anjali's elderly servant answered the door with a shuffle of slippers, but today the door swung open with a sudden swish, revealing Anjali herself.

She stood in the doorway, casual yet somehow striking. Manohar's eyes widened without him meaning to. She wore a pair of denim shorts that seemed to go on forever and a sleeveless blue T-shirt that clung to her frame, emphasising her sun-kissed skin. It wasn't that he hadn't seen her in casual clothes before, but today—today was different.

"Hi, Sir," Anjali greeted him, her tone light and mischievous. There was a sparkle in her eyes, something he hadn't noticed before.

He cleared his throat, suddenly feeling out of place. "Where's your servant?" he managed to ask, but his voice seemed too distant, as though it didn't belong to him.

Anjali's lips curled into a knowing smile. "He's gone to visit a relative. He won't be back until midnight." Her words lingered in the air, charged with an unfamiliar tension.

They made their way inside and as usual, Manohar took his seat at the table. But the atmosphere felt different. Anjali brought him a glass of water–her movements graceful, her presence somehow more intense than before. He sipped from the glass, hoping the cool liquid would calm the sudden restlessness creeping into his chest.

Opening the textbook, Manohar launched into his explanation of the reproductive system. But even as his voice remained steady, his thoughts kept drifting. Anjali's gaze was fixed on him, her attention unblinking, and it was enough to make his palms break into a sweat.

"I have a question, Sir," she interrupted in a low voice, filled with curiosity. The question that followed sent an immediate heat rushing to Manohar's face. It wasn't inappropriate, per se, but it certainly bordered on the edge of what was acceptable in a student-teacher relationship.

Manohar stumbled over words, flipping through the textbook in search of something to bring them back to the comfort of academia. He underlined a section with perhaps a little too much force. "Please read this carefully," he instructed, trying to keep the conversation on track.

Anjali, however, wasn't deterred. Her eyes flickered from the book to his face, her expression no longer one of curiosity but something more daring. "No, Sir," she whispered, her voice softer now, charged with an intensity that made the room feel smaller. "Can you show me... what it really feels like?"

Anjali rose gracefully from her chair, her every movement soft yet deliberate, as if drawn towards Manohar by an invisible thread. Her eyes filled with a quiet craving, never leaving his face as she closed the space between them. Each step she took seemed to carry the weight of emotions she had long kept hidden, now threatening to spill over.

She stood before him so close that he could feel the faint warmth of her presence. She paused. Her hands hovered uncertainly, trembling ever so slightly before she brought them together as if clasping an invisible hope. Her look searched his, tender and imploring, as though her very soul was reaching out to his.

Anjali widened her arms, her eyes burning with an unspoken intensity, and pulled him into her embrace with undeniable force. Before Manohar could react, her lips captured his in a deep, intense kiss, her breath mingling with his as time seemed to dissolve around them. She held him tight, her fingers digging into his back, as if afraid he might slip away. The kiss was not just passionate—it was desperate, claiming, filled with a hunger that had been simmering beneath the surface for far too long. She refused to let go, pouring every ounce of longing, every suppressed desire into the moment, making sure he felt the depth of her need.

"Sir," she murmured, her voice carrying a note of vulnerability that made his heart tighten. There was no mistaking the silent plea in her expression—a delicate blend of hope and the courage to bear her heart. She didn't need to say more; the air between them was charged with unspoken but deeply felt words.

The actions hung between them, heavy and physical. Manohar froze, staring at her in disbelief. He had never been in a situation like this before. It felt as if the very air around them had thickened. The sun streaming through the window was now too warm, and the room was suddenly stuffy.

Manohar's mind raced. He couldn't make sense of what had just happened. Anjali, the student he had been helping for weeks, had crossed a line he hadn't thought possible. He quickly stood up, putting some distance between them. "Anjali, this is not acceptable," he said, his voice firm, though his heart was pounding in his chest. "I am your teacher, and there is a boundary that must be respected."

Her smile only widened, a mischievous glint in her eyes. "Oh, come on, Sir," she said playfully, clearly unfazed. "Don't be so tense. I was just kidding. We're both grown-ups here, and you're such a good teacher. Why make a big deal out of it?"

Manohar's face hardened as he processed her words. This wasn't just a misunderstanding—this was blatant disrespect. He had come here with the intention of helping her with her studies, and now he was confronted with this. The situation left him feeling angry and betrayed.

"Anjali," he said, his voice sharp and unyielding, "teaching is not a game. What you suggested crosses every line of decency. I am here to help you learn. That's it. Nothing more. And I will not tolerate behaviour like this."

For a moment, Anjali's expression faltered. It was as though she realised she had gone too far. But instead of offering an apology, she simply shrugged, her arms crossing over her chest. "I don't see why you're making such a big deal of it. I thought you were more open-minded."

Manohar clenched his fists, trying to suppress the wave of frustration that surged through him. "This isn't about being open-minded. This is about professionalism. Integrity. Respect. You are my student, and I am your tutor. That's the only relationship we have. If you can't understand that, then maybe I shouldn't be coming here anymore."

He turned to leave, but as his hand reached the door knob, Anjali's voice softened, holding an edge of desperation. "Wait, Sir," she called. "Please don't go. I'm sorry." She took a hesitant step towards him, her earlier boldness replaced with something almost pleading. "I didn't mean to make you uncomfortable. I just—"

Manohar raised a hand to stop her. "Anjali, I think it's best if we end the session here today. I need some time to think about whether I want to continue tutoring you."

Without waiting for a response, he left the flat in a whirlwind. As he walked through the lavish corridors of the building, everything around him seemed unfamiliar and alien. The tension from the earlier confrontation still hung in the air, and he couldn't shake the thought of Simran. In comparison to Anjali's behaviour, Simran seemed like a breath of fresh air.

As he stepped outside into the cool evening air, Manohar took a deep breath, trying to clear his mind. One thing was certain: no amount of prestige or wealth could ever make him compromise his values. What had just happened crossed a line, and as he walked back to his modest room, he knew he needed to reassess everything—his priorities, his boundaries, and perhaps even his future in tutoring.

Manohar lay wide awake in his cramped room that night, his mind racing in a frenzy of confusion and frustration. The events of the day kept replaying, each moment more jarring than the last. Anjali's behaviour had left him feeling unsettled in ways he couldn't fully articulate. The respect he had always tried to uphold in his role as a teacher felt broken, shattered by the audacity of what had transpired. This wasn't just about a student crossing a line—it was about trust, professionalism, and boundaries being violated in a way he hadn't been prepared for.

The silence of the night seemed to press down on him, thick and suffocating, and he knew there was only one person he needed to confront—Simran. The very person who had recommended Anjali for tutoring, whose judgement he had trusted. He had always admired Simran's sincerity, but now, in the wake of this unsettling encounter, doubt crept in.

How could she not have known what kind of person Anjali was? How could she not have foreseen what had happened?

❋   ❋   ❋

The next morning, though still clouded by a sense of betrayal, Manohar decided he had to speak to Simran. His mind was a swirl of unresolved questions and anger, but he couldn't carry this weight alone. He had trusted her, and now he needed answers.

As he walked towards Simran's house, the quiet streets seemed to contrast his internal turmoil. The warmth of the sun, usually so comforting, felt almost oppressive. His footsteps were heavy, each one an echo of the frustration building within him. When he finally arrived, Simran greeted him with her usual warm smile, unaware of the storm that was brewing in his chest. Manohar didn't have the heart for pleasantries today.

"Simran," he said, his tone clipped and urgent. "We need to talk."

Simran's smile faltered, and her brow furrowed as she noticed the tension in his face. "Sure, Sir. What's the matter?" she asked, her voice laced with concern.

Manohar wasted no time. "Why did you recommend Anjali to me? Didn't you know what kind of person she is?"

Simran blinked in surprise, her eyes wide with confusion. "What do you mean? Anjali... she's my friend. I thought she needed help, and I thought you could—"

"Help?" Manohar interrupted, his frustration boiling over. "She didn't need help, Simran. She disrespected me. She crossed boundaries I never thought a student would. I went to her house to teach her, but she treated it as an excuse for romance. She crossed a line..."

Simran's face paled as she processed his words, her shock evident. "Sir, I... I didn't know. I never thought she would—"

"That's the problem, Simran!" Manohar's voice wavered with emotion. "You didn't think. You trusted me with someone who doesn't respect the values I stand for. I've always prided myself on maintaining respect with my students and what she did... it was completely unacceptable."

Simran's eyes filled with guilt, her voice trembling as she spoke. "Sir, I'm so sorry. I had no idea Anjali would behave like that. She never showed that side to me."

Manohar could see the sincerity in her eyes, but his anger hadn't subsided. "I didn't want to put you in this position, but I had to tell you. You need to understand how serious this is."

Simran lowered her gaze, her voice barely above a whisper. "I understand, Sir. I'm really sorry. I never would have introduced her to you if I thought this would happen."

A heavy silence filled the room as Manohar's words settled between them. Simran had meant well, of that he was sure, but her friend's actions had put him in an impossible situation. Manohar let out a deep sigh, trying to collect his thoughts and calm the storm inside him. "Simran," he said quietly, "I don't blame you entirely. But you need to understand how important this is to me. I can't compromise on my principles. Not for anyone."

Simran nodded, her voice barely audible as she whispered, "I understand, Sir. I'm sorry."

With that, Manohar turned to leave. The weight of the conversation still hung heavy in the air, and he knew that while Simran's remorse was genuine, things had changed between them. "I'll see you tomorrow for our regular session," he said, his voice lacking its usual warmth as he walked out the door.

✳   ✳   ✳

But just as he was stepping outside, the phone rang at Simran's house. She picked it up and called out, "Sir, your landlord wants to speak with you." It was a call from the landowner.

"Manohar," the voice on the other end was urgent. "Anjali's father just called me. He wants to meet with you immediately. I suggest you hurry to Anjali's house right away."

Manohar's stomach twisted. He had already been planning to tell Anjali's parents that he couldn't continue tutoring her after what had happened, but now it seemed they wanted to have their say first. Without hesitation, he headed in the direction of Anjali's house, bracing himself for the conversation that awaited him.

When he arrived, the atmosphere was thick with tension. Anjali's father was seated in the living room, his expression harsh and unyielding. The air was charged, and for a moment, no one spoke. Finally, it was Anjali's father, Mr. Saxena, who broke the silence.

"Manohar," he said, his voice low and deliberate, "I'm sure you're aware that my daughter has been under your care. But I need to understand what happened."

Manohar's heart sank. He had known this confrontation was coming, but hearing those words spoken aloud made it all the more real. The uneasy silence stretched on as he prepared to explain his side of the story, unsure of where this conversation would lead.

Manohar's heart was pounding. Every nerve in his body felt alive with tension, yet he remained still, trying to steady his breath. The decision had been made, but the weight of it hung heavily around him, threatening to suffocate him with each passing second. Anjali's father sat across from him, his eyes dark with suspicion, and beside him, Anjali, who appeared as if she had been struck by a bolt of lightning, her face a mix of confusion and disbelief.

"Manohar, I've heard troubling things," Anjali's father said, his voice stern. "I need to know what's going on between you and my daughter."

Manohar's throat went dry. The words he had rehearsed seemed to evaporate the moment he heard the question. He had known this conversation was inevitable, but the intensity of the moment was unlike anything he had prepared for. His eyes flickered towards Anjali, whose gaze remained fixed on him, not with the admiration she once held, but with something far more complicated.

"Your daughter," Manohar began, his voice surprisingly steady despite the storm raging inside him, "is a bright student. There's no doubt about that. But biology… It's a struggle for her. She keeps repeating the same mistakes, and no matter what I do, I can't seem to break through. I'm afraid I can't continue tutoring her."

The words felt hollow as they left his lips. He could feel the weight of the unspoken truth lingering just beneath the surface, but he couldn't bring himself to voice it. The incident with Anjali, the boundary she had crossed, was something he couldn't expose to her parents. Not now, not like this.

Anjali's father leaned forward, his eyes narrowing. "Biology? That's why you can't teach her anymore?" His tone was sharp, laced with suspicion. "You're telling me she isn't capable enough for you to continue?"

Manohar fought the urge to flinch. "Yes, Sir. I've tried, but the progress isn't there. It's frustrating. I don't want to waste your time or money if I can't make a difference."

Anjali's lips parted, but no words came out at first. She seemed almost frozen in place as if the ground beneath her had shifted without warning. Finally, she spoke, her voice barely above a whisper. "But, Sir, you never mentioned any of this before. I've been trying hard. I thought I was improving…"

Manohar didn't look at her. He couldn't. If he met her gaze, the facade he had so carefully constructed might crumble. Instead, he focused on her father's expectant stare.

"I couldn't bring myself to tell you sooner," Manohar replied, the words tasting bitter on his tongue. "I kept hoping things would get better, but they didn't. I've come to realise that I'm not the right tutor for her."

The silence that followed was thick, suffocating. Anjali's mother, who had remained quiet until now, spoke up, her voice soft but sharp with concern. "Are you sure there's nothing else, Mr. Manohar? We've always heard such good things about you from Anjali. She's always praising your teaching."

Manohar's pulse quickened, but he remained composed, forcing a smile that didn't quite reach his eyes. "Ma'am, I assure you, there's nothing else. I've just reached a point where I believe it's best for Anjali to find a tutor who can help her in a way I can't."

Anjali's father leaned back in his chair, his gaze unwavering. "I see. But let me make this clear, Manohar, if there's more to this, I'll find out. We trusted you with our daughter's education."

Manohar nodded, his throat tight. "Of course, Sir. I understand. I only want what's best for Anjali."

As he turned to leave, he could feel the weight of Anjali's gaze pressing against him like an invisible force. Her silence, her unresolved emotions, were like a silent plea for him to speak the truth, but he couldn't. Not here, not now. With a final nod to her parents, he stepped out into the cool air, his thoughts swirling like a storm inside his head.

Outside, the world felt both distant and too close at once. As he walked away, he couldn't shake the feeling that he had left something unresolved. There was the relief of escaping the confrontation, but there was also the gnawing guilt of the secret he had kept. The truth had stayed buried, but for how long?

✳ ✳ ✳

Simran, back at her own home, couldn't push the unease away. The incident with Anjali worried her like a persistent itch she couldn't scratch. She had always known Anjali to be carefree, even reckless at times, but this... this was different. It wasn't just the flirtation or the teasing; it was the violation of boundaries that Simran had always held sacred. Anjali had crossed a line, and now Simran felt caught in the crossfire.

She sat in her room, textbooks scattered across her desk, but her mind was miles away. Her thoughts raced in a chaotic whirlwind, circling around Anjali's betrayal, her own feelings for Manohar, and the weight of everything that had transpired. "How could she?" Simran muttered under her breath. "How could Anjali do that to him?"

Every conversation she had ever had with Anjali now played in her mind, each one laced with an unsettling undertone. Anjali had always spoken highly of Manohar, but now Simran wondered if it had been more than just admiration. Had Anjali always seen Manohar as a challenge? A conquest? The thought sent a chill running down her spine.

Anjali had tried to use Manohar's kindness and professionalism as a weakness to manipulate him for her own gain. And Simran—Simran felt torn. She had been loyal to her friend for so long, but this... this was different. There was something bigger at stake now. Something she couldn't ignore any longer.

"Every person has a weakness," Simran recalled, a chill running down her spine. The words echoed in her mind like a warning, one that she had once dismissed but now understood all too well. Anjali had exploited that weakness, and Simran knew deep down that if she wasn't careful, she too could be drawn into the same web.

She sat on the edge of her bed, her hands trembling. What if Anjali tried again? What if she came to Simran, trying to pull her into her lies? Simran could already feel the pressure mounting, the pull between loyalty and love—her love for Manohar, the man who had always treated her with such kindness and respect.

The weight of her feelings seemed to bear down on her all at once. She had always hoped that Manohar would see her for who she truly was—that he would one day notice the quiet affection she had harboured for him all these years. But now, with everything unfolding the way it was, she wondered if that moment would ever come. Would Anjali's actions push Simran to finally act on her feelings? Or would she be forced to watch from the side-lines as the man she loved drifted further away?

Simran sat in her room, staring at her textbooks, but her mind was far from the equations and formulas that filled the pages. It wasn't the looming board exams that disturbed her, but the storm that had been brewing between her and Anjali, the betrayal, and the confusion about Manohar. The air around her felt thick with unspoken words, and the question that refused to leave her mind echoed repeatedly: What should I do?

Her gaze fell on the neatly stacked books in front of her, but it was as if they had no relevance now. The realisation of Anjali's actions had shaken her to the core, not just for what had happened, but for what it revealed. Simran was not like Anjali. She didn't use people. She didn't manipulate. She respected Manohar far too much to treat him like a pawn in some game. But the fear—no, the gut-wrenching certainty—that Anjali might succeed where she had been patient, where she had remained silent, gnawed at her.

Her fingers traced the edges of the book, but her thoughts were elsewhere. The idea of Anjali, with her charm and recklessness, taking what Simran could never have was too much.

"Do I just wait?" Simran whispered to herself, her voice barely a breath in the stillness of the room. Her words hung in the air unanswered.

She wrestled with a deep, consuming conflict: her growing love for Manohar and the panic of losing him. The absurdity of it all, the reckless way Anjali had thrown their worlds into chaos, left her wondering if love could truly survive the tide of jealousy, betrayal, and miscommunication. Could it withstand the storm of doubt that swirled between them?

❋　❋　❋

The next day was no better. Simran had barely slept, her mind racing with a thousand thoughts. Every time she closed her eyes, it was as though the scene with Anjali played over again, taunting her. She needed answers. She had to confront her friend, to clear the air, to understand what had happened, or at least to seek the truth she felt lingering between the words both spoken and unspoken. The bell rang at school, signalling the end of the day. As the students flooded out of the classroom, Simran spotted Anjali near the courtyard, laughing with friends.

Simran took a deep breath. There was no turning back now. She walked over, her face set with purpose. "Anjali, can we talk for a minute?" Her voice was firm, more serious than usual, and Anjali, noticing the change, looked up, eyebrows raised.

"Sure, what's up?" Anjali replied, though there was an edge of uncertainty in her voice.

They stepped aside, finding a quiet corner beneath a sprawling tree, away from the hustle and bustle of the courtyard. The conversation that had been simmering for days was now unavoidable.

Simran wasted no time. "Anjali," she began, her voice cutting through the air with sharp intensity, "Why did you do it? Why did you make such a mess of things with my sir?"

Anjali blinked, a playful smirk still on her lips, though there was a flicker of discomfort in her eyes. "Mess? Come on, Simran. It was just a joke. Some harmless fun," she said, brushing it off as though it meant nothing.

Simran's temper flared. "Harmless fun?" Her voice rose, frustration pouring out. "Anjali, you're a young girl, and you need to know your boundaries. Do you even realise what you could have done? You could have ruined his career. This isn't something one takes lightly."

For the first time, Anjali's confident demeanour faltered. She looked down at her shoes, shifting uncomfortably. "I know... I know," she muttered. "But I didn't mean it like that. I wasn't thinking clearly."

Simran didn't back down, stepping closer, her voice hardening. "It doesn't matter what you intended. What matters is that you crossed a line. You don't just play around with someone's reputation, Anjali. My sir deserves respect, not a joke at his expense."

Anjali's bravado crumbled further, and she looked genuinely remorseful, her usual levity replaced with an unfamiliar vulnerability. "Simran, I didn't mean for it to go this far. I didn't plan for any of this. But I swear I think Manohar Sir is great. He's... different. He handled everything so well, so calmly. He didn't even tell my parents what really happened. He protected me even when I didn't deserve it."

Simran's eyes narrowed. There was something in Anjali's voice, something deeper than simple admiration. "Do you admire him? Or is it something more than that?" Simran asked, her tone probing, more suspicious now.

Anjali laughed nervously, her usual self-assurance slipping. "Oh no, Simran, don't get any ideas. It's not like that! I don't love him in that way," she said quickly, her cheeks flushing slightly. "I just... I really admire how smart he is. He's so mature, so composed. He's not like the other guys we know. He's different."

Simran's heart twisted painfully. She didn't want to admit it, but deep down, she feared there was more to Anjali's feelings than she was willing to admit.

"So what is it that you want, Anjali?" Simran's voice softened, but there was still an edge to it. "You know how I feel about him. You know he means a lot to me."

Anjali met Simran's gaze, her expression now solemn, her words more measured. "Simran, I swear, I don't want to get in the way. You've always liked him. You've always had feelings for him. But listen, if you really love him, you should go for it. Don't let him slip away. He's too good to lose."

Simran stood frozen, staring at her friend. The words hung between them like a storm cloud. Anjali, the very person who had tried to pull Manohar away, was now telling her to fight for him. It felt wrong and twisted, but Simran knew there was a bitter truth in what Anjali said. If she didn't act soon, she could lose him forever.

"I don't know, Anjali," Simran finally whispered, the weight of the situation pressing down on her. "I just don't know."

Anjali gave a sad smile. She said softly but in a matter-of-fact tone, "You'd better decide soon, Simran. Men like him don't stay single forever."

Simran nodded, her heart heavy with indecision. One thing was certain, though—time was running out. If she didn't act soon, she risked losing Manohar forever.

At the same time, her own future loomed large. She was eighteen now, with the board exams on the horizon. The pressure was immense. She knew she couldn't afford any distractions, but the pull of her feelings for Manohar was undeniable. And then there was Anjali's presence, an ever-present shadow in her thoughts. Simran couldn't let that stop her, though. Her future, her career, had to come first.

Manohar was wrestling with his own emotions. The situation with Anjali had rattled him, and though he had considered walking away, he couldn't bring himself to. Mrs. Malhotra's trust in him had kept him grounded. He continued to show up for Simran's tutoring sessions, focusing on her future while burying his own confusion.

✳　✳　✳

"Simran," he said one evening, his voice calm yet insistent, "now is the time to revise hard. The syllabus is finished, but if you need more time, I'm here. Just focus, and don't let what happened with Anjali distract you."

Simran glanced up, her smile faint but knowing. He wasn't just talking about different subjects. He was reminding her to stay on course, not just with her studies, but with her life. She knew what he meant: focus on your goals, on your future. And yet, with every word, the struggle inside her grew. Could she truly separate her emotions from her ambitions? Could she truly keep the fear of losing him at bay, all while striving for the life she had dreamed of?

The words lingered in Simran's mind long after Manohar had spoken them. She had always respected him—not just for his intellect, but for the way he lived his life with quiet integrity and a no-nonsense approach. Unlike others, his words weren't filled with empty encouragement or clichéd optimism. They were grounded, real, and, above all, practical. It wasn't about offering her false hope; it was about helping her find the strength within herself to push forward. His belief in her was not just a passing comment; it was a call to rise above the distractions and prove to herself that she was capable of far more than she realised.

"Yes, Sir," Simran said, her voice firm, almost resolute. "I can do it. I'm ready to work very hard." The words, simple as they were, felt like a promise she made not just to him, but to herself.

Manohar looked at her closely, his gaze softening as he noticed the seriousness in her eyes. He knew this wasn't just about academics for Simran. It was a battle that reached much deeper—against the uncertainty in her heart, against the chaos of emotions that often clouded her mind. She was navigating the storm of young love, academic pressure and the pressure to succeed in the face of personal doubt. As her tutor, he had seen her in moments of self-doubt, but he had also witnessed her quiet strength. And in that moment, he knew Simran had the resilience to overcome any obstacle, even if she didn't fully believe it herself.

Simran sat back down at her desk, the familiar scent of books surrounding her. She flipped through the pages of physics and mathematics, each formula and concept now seeming less like an overwhelming task and more like a step towards something bigger. For the first time in weeks, she felt the weight of the textbooks lift off her shoulders. This wasn't just about passing exams anymore. This was about discovering what she was truly made of. It wasn't about pleasing Manohar, or anyone else. It was about proving to herself that she had the strength to face whatever came her way.

The following weeks were gruelling. Simran threw herself into her studies with a focus that bordered on obsession. Hours blurred into each other as she studied for eight to ten hours each day. Manohar, ever patient and committed, made time to meet her twice a day to clarify doubts, particularly in mathematics, where she still struggled. But no matter how hard she worked, there was an unease that refused to leave her. It was a nagging fear that despite her best efforts, something would go wrong—that failure was just a step behind, waiting to catch her off guard.

And then, there was the shadow of Anjali's incident, lingering in the corners of her thoughts. During the quiet moments when she should have been focused on her studies, the memory of that day would creep back in. The anxiety over Anjali's behaviour, the unsettling question of whether it had caused severe damage, gnawed at her constantly. Simran found herself questioning not only her academic abilities but her emotional resilience as well. How could she focus on her future when the echoes of that incident kept distracting her?

One evening, as Simran sat hunched over her textbooks, trying to solve a particularly tricky maths problem, Manohar noticed her growing anxiety. He could see it in her eyes— the same unease that had haunted her since the day of the incident. Sensing the weight of her thoughts, he broke the silence.

"Simran," he said gently, his voice calm yet firm, "you've prepared well. You shouldn't worry so much."

Simran didn't look up immediately. She kept her eyes on the page, but her frown deepened. "Sir," she said softly, "What if I can't solve these problems? What if I fail?"

Manohar's gaze didn't waver. He knew the pressure Simran was under, and he also knew she needed more than just a reassuring nod from him. She needed a reason to believe in herself, to trust in her own abilities.

"Don't think like that," Manohar replied, his tone measured but filled with confidence. "You've worked hard, and I've seen how much you've improved in maths. You'll do just fine."

But Simran was persistent, her doubts outweighing his reassurances. "But, Sir, I'm not confident in myself. I keep feeling like something will go wrong."

Manohar paused, his eyes thoughtful for a moment. Then, as if to dispel her fears, he shared something personal—a story from his own past.

"When I was preparing for my board exams," he began, "my father didn't believe I could get a first class. He had his doubts about me. But you know who believed in me? My tutor."

Simran looked up at him, intrigued. She could sense that there was more to this story than just another tale of academic achievement.

"We were twelve students under his guidance," Manohar continued, a faint smile playing at the corner of his mouth, "but he predicted that only five of us would get a first class. And, do you know what? He was right. I was one of the five."

Simran's curiosity was piqued. She leaned forward, her attention now fully on him.

"Do you know why I wanted to get that first class so badly?" Manohar asked, his voice softening with a touch of nostalgia. "In my school, there was a tradition. The names of the first-class students were engraved on a board, dating back to 1952. Every time I passed that board, I saw the names of my grandfather and uncle. But my father's name wasn't there. He had only gotten second class, and he always told me—half-proud, half-regretful—that he hoped

I would carry on the family legacy. It became my challenge, my goal—to see my name on that board."

Simran sat in silence for a moment, reflecting on the determination that had driven Manohar to success despite the doubts surrounding him.

"So, Sir," she said, her voice steady, "you took on that challenge and succeeded."

Manohar nodded. "Exactly. And so can you, Simran. You've prepared well. Now, it's time to accept your challenge and believe in yourself. You're ready."

Simran's gaze returned to her books, but something had changed. The story Manohar had shared resonated deeply with her. If he could rise above the challenges and succeed, then so could she. She wasn't just studying to pass exams anymore. She was studying to honour the strength that had been there all along—the strength she was beginning to believe in.

Chapter 13

BOARD EXAM

The morning of the exam arrived with an air of quiet anticipation, thick with nerves and the weight of expectations. Simran, dressed in her school uniform, stood by the door, her hands trembling slightly as she clutched her exam hall ticket. Her mother was beside her, adjusting her scarf and offering a reassuring smile. But the nerves wouldn't leave, swirling in her stomach, making her feel like she could hardly breathe. It was the day that could shape her future, and the pressure of it felt almost unbearable.

As they were about to leave, there was an unexpected knock at the door. Simran's heart skipped a beat. She wasn't expecting anyone, certainly not at this hour. But to her surprise, it was Manohar standing on the doorstep, his usual calm presence as steady as ever.

"Auntie, can I drop Simran off at the exam centre?" he asked, his tone gentle, with that same steady confidence that always put her at ease.

Mrs. Malhotra blinked, caught off guard by the sudden act of kindness. "Of course, *beta*. That's very thoughtful of you," she replied warmly, a soft smile lighting up her face.

Simran, already anxious about the exam, felt a wave of surprise wash over her. She hadn't expected her tutor to show up and offer to drop her. She glanced at her mother, who smiled encouragingly and gently nudged her to accept. Within moments, they were in an auto-rickshaw, headed towards the exam centre, with Manohar sitting beside her, offering last-minute advice that, despite her nerves, she hung on to.

"Simran," Manohar said, his voice calm and steady, "start with the 5-mark questions. Those are your strongest areas. Once you've got those done, move on to the 3, 2, and 1-mark questions. But remember, time management is key. And most importantly, always check your answers before submitting them. A small mistake could cost you valuable marks."

Simran listened, her mind trying to absorb every word. His calmness, like a steady anchor in a storm, eased some of the chaos in her mind. She nodded, mentally rehearsing her strategy as the auto-rickshaw rumbled on towards the exam centre.

They arrived an hour early. As Simran stepped out, she saw her friends gathered in small huddles, their conversations a mix of anxiety and last-minute revisions. Among them was Anjali, standing tall, her usual confidence unwavering. As soon as she spotted Simran and Manohar, she walked over with her usual mischievous grin.

"Good morning, Sir!" Anjali greeted Manohar, her eyes sparkling with playful energy.

Manohar smiled politely, although he was well aware of Anjali's teasing nature. "How are you, Anjali?"

"No problems in maths, but I still have some doubts about biology," Anjali said with a wink, her tone light-hearted but with a hint of challenge.

Simran, watching the exchange, felt a subtle wave of annoyance but didn't let it show. She had no time for distractions today. She turned to Manohar, her voice steady despite the nervousness creeping up again.

"Sir, you can go now," Simran said, trying to keep her focus. "I need to revise."

Manohar, however, shook his head, his gaze unwavering. "No, I'll wait. You're about to face something that could change your life, Simran. These 180 minutes matter. So stay focused."

His words, though simple, grounded her in the moment. Despite the rising tension and the buzzing noise of other students, Simran felt a sense of calm that only his presence seemed to bring. She gave him a small nod, then made her way into the exam hall. Manohar's reassuring nod stayed with her as she disappeared through the doors.

Outside, Manohar walked to a nearby park, seeking the shade of a tree. The sun was already burning with the kind of heat that made everything feel heavy, but he didn't mind. His mind was with Simran. He couldn't help but think of her every second, wishing her the strength to do her best. He sat quietly, praying for her success, as the minutes ticked by in silence.

The exam finally ended, and students began trickling out of the hall, their faces a mixture of emotions. Some looked triumphant, others downcast. Simran, however, walked out with a thoughtful expression, unsure whether to feel elated or disheartened. She had done her best, but the uncertainty of the outcome gnawed at her.

As she stepped outside into the heat, she had expected Manohar to have already left. She was just about to hail an auto when she heard her name being called.

"Simran!"

She turned, surprised to see Manohar standing some distance away, his hand raised in greeting. She couldn't help but smile at the sight of him, his steady presence still a source of reassurance.

"Sir, you're still here?" Simran asked, her voice tinged with disbelief.

"Of course," Manohar replied with a smile. "How did it go? Show me the question paper."

Simran handed him the question paper, her fingers still slightly trembling. Manohar took it from her and began scanning through the questions with a practised eye. After a few moments, he looked up, his expression confident, almost certain.

"You'll score more than 80 percent in maths, I'm sure of it," he said, his voice steady and filled with unwavering belief.

Simran stared at him, surprised by his confidence. The anxiety that had gripped her all day began to lift, replaced by a quiet sense of pride. Perhaps, just perhaps, Manohar's faith in her was not misplaced after all. And as they walked together towards the waiting auto, the weight of the day finally seemed to ease, replaced by a sense of hope she hadn't allowed herself to feel before.

Simran shook her head, still unsure of how she had performed. "I don't think so, Sir. I made a few mistakes," she said, her voice tinged with doubt.

Manohar, however, offered her a reassuring smile, the kind that conveyed quiet confidence. "You will. That's my bet," he said, his belief unwavering.

Simran felt the warmth of his faith in her seep into her heart. For the first time that day, she began to believe in herself, just a little more. His simple words, full of conviction, lifted her spirits, making her realise that perhaps her self-doubt wasn't as justified as she thought.

As the other exam papers came closer, Manohar's dedication to Simran's success grew even more evident. He took extra care with her tuition, extending their hours, sometimes staying late into the evening, determined to ensure that every question was answered, every doubt was cleared, and every topic was thoroughly reviewed. His commitment to Simran's future never wavered, and it didn't go unnoticed by her parents.

One evening, as they sat around the dinner table, Mrs. Malhotra couldn't help but express her gratitude. Stirring her *dal* thoughtfully, she said, "Really, I feel like we've been blessed to have someone like Manohar looking after Simran.

It's like we got a godsend. He's so devoted to her success, so caring about every little detail."

Mr. Malhotra nodded in agreement, setting his plate down and leaning back in his chair. "I've always told you, haven't I? Particularly, some Bihari's are very sharp-minded. I knew from the beginning he'd be a great teacher. People from that region often have a real hunger for knowledge and success."

Mrs. Malhotra, while appreciative, wasn't one to make broad generalisations. "Sharp? Yes, Manohar certainly is. But don't get carried away. Not all of them are so hardworking or intelligent," she countered with a chuckle, folding her arms. "We've met others before who didn't impress me much."

"True, true," Mr. Malhotra said, taking a sip of his tea. "But look at him. He's not just intelligent; he's got discipline. That's what sets him apart. He's dedicated to Simran's education, and not many tutors would go to the lengths he has. Most just come, teach, and leave. But this boy, he's different. He even suggested a diet plan for her—who does that?"

Mrs. Malhotra smiled, a touch of admiration in her voice. "Yes, that was unexpected. He's genuinely concerned about her well-being. He asked me the other day if Simran was eating enough protein. He says proper nutrition will help her focus better. Can you imagine?"

Mr. Malhotra raised an eyebrow, clearly impressed. "That's something. He's thinking beyond just studies. I don't think I've ever met a tutor who cared that much. He's looking out for her future in more ways than one."

"You know," Mrs. Malhotra mused, "there's something so genuine about him. He doesn't have any of that arrogance you see in some of these Delhi tutors. He's simple, down-to-earth, and truly wants Simran to succeed. He's like a part of the family now."

"Exactly," Mr. Malhotra agreed, setting his cup down. "And that's why I trust him completely. He doesn't just do this for the money. He's got integrity. A rare quality these days."

Mrs. Malhotra smiled softly, her heart swelling with appreciation. "It's true. And you know, Simran has never had this kind of confidence in her studies before. She's taken to heart everything he's taught her. I can see it in her."

"Well, let's hope all this hard work pays off," Mr. Malhotra said, leaning back with a satisfied smile. "With Manohar's guidance and Simran's determination, I have no doubt she'll do well."

The two of them fell into a comfortable silence, the weight of their shared gratitude hanging in the air. Manohar had become more than just a tutor to them—he had earned their trust and admiration and had become a true part of their family. His impact on Simran's future had been profound, and they both knew it.

After an intense month of exams, Simran's final papers were completed. Manohar had been there for every single one, offering advice, encouragement, and a steady presence before each session. Now, with the ordeal behind her, Simran felt a mixture of relief and exhaustion.

"Sir, are you coming over to my house now that the exams are done?" she asked, a hopeful smile tugging at her lips, clearly longing for some time to unwind.

"Why?" Manohar replied with a playful grin. "You're ready to start preparing for your next class already? Getting a head start on the curriculum?"

Simran let out a small laugh, the tension in her body easing for the first time in days. "No, Sir. I think I deserve a little relaxation first. The next class can wait."

Manohar's smile softened, understanding her need for a break. "Of course," he agreed, his tone genuine. "You've worked hard. It's important to take some time, relax and refresh your mind before the next innings begins."

Simran nodded, already feeling the weight of the past few weeks lifting off her shoulders. "What do you suggest I do, Sir?"

Manohar thought for a moment before responding, his eyes twinkling with a hint of mischief. "Well, I think you've earned a good rest. Take some time for yourself—do something that makes you happy. Watch a movie, read a book, or just take a nap. You've earned it."

Simran grinned at his suggestion. "I think I'll do just that," she said, feeling lighter than she had in weeks. The exams were over, and for the first time in a long while, she could truly relax.

"Why not visit a hill station or spend some time at a relative's house?" Manohar suggested with a hint of warmth in his voice. "A change of scenery might do you good."

Simran paused, her gaze thoughtful as she turned the idea over in her mind. Then, with a spark of hope in her eyes, she looked at him and asked, "Sir, would you go with me? It would be fun to travel together."

Manohar smiled, but there was a trace of regret in his expression. He gently shook his head. "I wish I could, Simran, but I've got some competitive exams coming up. I need to focus on those. How could I take time off now?"

Simran's face fell slightly, but she quickly recovered. She understood. Manohar, too, had dreams, goals, and responsibilities. She couldn't expect him to pause his own ambitions just to accompany her on a trip. "I understand, Sir," she said, her voice steady and warm. "I know how important your exams are."

A week later, Manohar decided to pay a visit to Simran's home. He had been thinking about how she might benefit from a small break to recharge after the intensity of her exams. Mrs. Malhotra welcomed him with her usual kindness, her eyes sparkling with gratitude for his continued care and attention towards Simran.

"*Beta*," Mrs. Malhotra said, offering him a cup of tea as they sat down in the living room, "Simran doesn't seem ready to go anywhere. She's been resting at home but doesn't want to visit anyone."

Manohar listened attentively, his mind already turning over solutions. "Aunty, I understand. But I truly believe that a short trip, even if it's just a weekend getaway, could do her a world of good. She's worked so hard, and now she needs to take a step back and refresh her mind before diving into her studies again."

Mrs. Malhotra sighed softly, glancing towards the door. There stood Simran, who had been quietly listening to their conversation, her head slightly bowed. "You know how she is, *beta*. She's so absorbed in her studies and even more so in her work with you. She's afraid that taking a break might disrupt her momentum."

Manohar offered a reassuring smile. "That's exactly why she needs this, Aunty. A fresh mind can make all the difference, especially when it's time to prepare for the next big challenge. Perhaps if you suggested visiting a relative, it wouldn't feel so much like she's stepping away from her goals."

Simran stepped into the room, her expression thoughtful. "I don't know... I've been so focused on my exams. Maybe a break isn't such a bad idea." She turned to her mother. "How about we visit Uncle in Chandigarh? I've been wanting to see my cousins there anyway."

Manohar's face lit up with encouragement. "That's the spirit, Simran. A few weeks in a new environment, surrounded by family, could be just what you need. When you come back, you'll be more than ready to take on the next step."

Simran smiled, feeling a sense of relief wash over her. It was as if the weight of the last few weeks had lifted slightly, just by imagining the change of place.

"Enjoy your time there, Simran," Manohar said, his voice filled with genuine care. "Make the most of it. Recharge, and when you're back, I know you'll be more focused than ever."

As they bid each other farewell, both Simran and Manohar knew that this short break was more than just a chance to relax. It was an opportunity for her to clear her mind and regain her energy, ready to face whatever the next academic challenge was in store for her. Manohar's belief in her was unwavering, and that trust would be there, guiding her even from a distance.

Chapter 14

TRIP TO CHANDIGARH

Simran arrived in Chandigarh early in the morning, stepping into the clean, well-planned city with its broad, tree-lined avenues and lush greenery. The city's well-planned grid layout, quiet roundabouts, and architectural precision were unlike the bustling chaos of Delhi. It felt like a breath of fresh air, a world apart from the crowded streets she was used to. Chandigarh's calmness felt soothing, yet it sparked a sense of unfamiliarity in Simran. The gardens, wide parks, and serene atmosphere gave her time to reflect on her life, away from the intensity of her board exams and the emotional whirlwind of her relationship with Manohar.

Simran reached her uncle's house, a modest but well-kept residence in a quiet sector of Chandigarh. Her uncle and aunt were both employed in private companies and their only daughter, Tinki, was in the 9th standard. Tinki, lively and inquisitive, greeted her at the door with a burst of questions.

"So, how were your exams, *didi*?" Tinki asked, her eyes sparkling with curiosity.

Simran smiled warmly but kept her response neutral. "Well, let's see what happens."

Tinki giggled. "You'll do great! Papa says you have a really good tutor. Will you send him here to Chandigarh to guide me? I need someone like that."

Simran hesitated for a moment, her thoughts flickering to Manohar. "He's busy with his exams, Tinki, so I don't think he can come here."

Tinki pouted playfully. "Okay, but *didi*, is he smart?"

Simran, caught off guard by the directness of the question, laughed. "Yes, he's very smart. He's... well, very dedicated and always willing to help. He's kind too, you know, like a mentor who genuinely cares about his students."

Tinki's eyes widened with curiosity. "It sounds like you like him a lot, *didi*. Is he your boyfriend or something?"

Simran's heart skipped a beat at the unexpected question. She was stumped, unable to find words, her face growing warm. "Why are you asking me that?" she finally managed to say.

Tinki shrugged innocently. "You've praised him a lot. It just sounded like you like him. Like how people talk about their boyfriends."

Simran's discomfort deepened as she scrambled to change the subject. However, their conversation had not gone unnoticed. Her aunt, overhearing the exchange, entered the room with a knowing smile. She sat down beside Simran, her eyes sparkling with gentle curiosity.

"Simran, what's this? I'm hearing about you and your tutor," her aunt asked in a teasing tone. "Your parents have praised him to us quite a lot. But what's the real story?"

Simran blushed, feeling cornered. She hadn't anticipated this level of scrutiny. "Nothing is going on, Aunty. He's just... well, he's a good person. My parents admire him because he's helped me a lot with my studies."

Her aunt raised an eyebrow, sensing that there was more to the story. Over the next few days, she would ask Simran more questions, gently coaxing out the truth, piece by piece. Simran eventually admitted what she had been hiding—not just to her aunt, but to herself. It wasn't just about Manohar's intelligence or dedication as a teacher. It was about the way he made her feel safe, cared for, and seen.

Her aunt listened thoughtfully, then smiled knowingly. "It's not just his intelligence you're drawn to, is it? It's the way he looks after you, the way he treats you with kindness."

Simran nodded, her heart heavy with the weight of her own realisation. She had fallen in love with her tutor, not only because of his brilliance, but because of the person he was—caring, patient, and someone who made her feel valued. This revelation, coming to light in the peaceful environment of her uncle's home, marked a turning point in Simran's emotional journey. Now, she had to decide what to do with those feelings.

In the evenings, she found herself in conversations with her aunt and uncle, often about her future. One evening, after dinner, Simran sat with her aunt in the living room while her uncle was reading the newspaper nearby. Her aunt initiated a conversation that Simran had been unconsciously avoiding.

"So, Simran," her aunt began, her tone both gentle and probing, "you've mentioned this tutor of yours, Manohar, quite a few times. Your parents also seem to speak highly of him."

Simran, a little taken aback, hesitated. "Yes, Aunty, he's been a great help, especially with my studies."

Her aunt gave her a knowing look, sensing there was more beneath the surface. "But is there something more between you two?" she asked carefully.

Simran's heart raced. She had always known she had feelings for Manohar, but discussing them openly felt daunting. "I... I don't know, Aunty. He's kind, intelligent, and has been so supportive. I've grown to admire him a lot."

Her uncle looked up from his paper, curious but not interrupting. Her aunt leaned closer, speaking softly. "Simran, it's natural to feel admiration for someone who has guided you, especially in such an important phase of your life. But admiration doesn't always mean love, and love—especially at your age—can be confusing."

Simran looked down, unsure of how to respond. Her feelings were genuine, but hearing her aunt's words made her realise how tangled they had become.

Her uncle finally chimed in, setting the newspaper aside. "Simran, your career is just beginning. You're smart and capable, and there's a whole world ahead of you. Falling in love is fine, but it shouldn't become the sole focus of your life, especially not now."

Simran glanced between her uncle and aunt, unsure of where the conversation was heading. Her aunt's expression softened. "Listen, I understand that caste and tradition don't matter to you and they shouldn't. But there's also the fact that you're just starting to figure out who you are. Love can be beautiful, but it can also be distracting when you're still figuring out your future."

Simran bit her lip, feeling the weight of their words. Her aunt continued, "I'm not saying Manohar isn't a good man. But ask yourself—do you know what you truly want? Or are you just drawn to him because he's been a stable presence in your life?"

Her uncle added, "This is your time to explore your potential, Simran. Education, career, personal growth— these are the things that will define your future. Don't limit yourself before you've even seen what you're capable of."

Simran sat in silence for a moment, letting her aunt's words sink in. Her aunt's voice became even gentler. "I want you to think about your goals. You've worked hard to get to where you are, and there's so much more you can achieve. Don't let your feelings for Manohar, however strong, derail your ambitions. Focus on your career first, and everything else will fall into place."

Finally, Simran spoke, her voice steady but reflective. "You're right, Aunty, Uncle. I've been so caught up in my feelings that I didn't think about what's best for me right now. I do need to focus on my career and on becoming someone I'm proud of before I can think about love."

Her aunt smiled, relieved that Simran understood. "That's the right attitude, dear. And if it's meant to be, love will find its way when the time is right."

Simran nodded, feeling a sense of clarity she hadn't felt before. She realised that her future held so many possibilities, and love, though important, wasn't the only thing that defined her journey. She was ready to put her energy into her studies and career, leaving the complexities of love for later.

❋   ❋   ❋

Simran had barely settled back into the rhythm of home after her trip to Chandigarh when a new kind of restlessness began to creep into her days. The results of her board exams were just around the corner, and the weight of uncertainty hung over her like an unspoken cloud. Sitting on the couch, she twirled the edge of her dupatta absentmindedly, her thoughts inevitably circling back to one person—her tutor, Manohar.

"Mum, have you seen Sir recently?" she asked, her voice laced with equal parts curiosity and nervousness.

Mrs. Malhotra looked up from her morning tea with a faint smile. "I ran into him at the market last week. He seemed his usual self—busy with his studies."

Simran hesitated, her fingers fidgeting. "Did he... um, ask about me?"

Mrs. Malhotra couldn't help but chuckle at the barely concealed anxiety in her daughter's tone. "Of course he did. He asked how you were doing and mentioned the results. He said they'd be out soon."

Simran's cheeks warmed as she nodded, unsure how to continue. Finally, she blurted out, "Mom, do you think he could check my results at school when they're out?"

Her mother raised an eyebrow, a playful glint in her eye. "Why don't you ask him yourself, *beta*?"

Simran quickly shook her head, her blush deepening. "No, Mum. Please, you ask him. I'd feel too awkward."

Mrs. Malhotra laughed softly. "Alright, alright. I'll talk to him. But don't be so shy. He always speaks highly of you."

The next morning, as the first rays of sunlight painted the sky, Mrs. Malhotra decided it was time. Pulling Simran along, they made their way to Manohar's modest flat. Standing at the door, she rang the bell, the sound echoing in the quiet of the early hour. A moment later, a sleepy face appeared on the balcony above.

"Good morning, Aunty," greeted one of Manohar's flatmates, stifling a yawn. "What brings you here so early?"

"We need to see Manohar. Can you call him?" Mrs. Malhotra asked.

The young man nodded and disappeared into the flat. Moments later, Manohar emerged from his room, his glasses slightly uneven and his shirt hastily buttoned. He looked both surprised and curious as he came down to greet them.

"Good morning, Aunty. Simran, you're back!" he said, his tone warm but tinged with curiosity.

Simran nodded, offering a small smile. "Yes, Sir. I got back a couple of days ago."

Manohar's gaze softened as he noticed her nervous demeanour. "How was your trip? Did you like Chandigarh?"

"It was nice," she replied quickly, clearly preoccupied.

Sensing her unease, Mrs. Malhotra spoke up. "Manohar *beta*, we came to ask if you could check Simran's results at school later today. She's feeling too anxious to go herself."

Manohar's brows lifted slightly in surprise, but he nodded without hesitation. "Of course, Aunty. I'd be happy to."

He turned to Simran, his voice gentle. "Would you like to come with me?"

Simran shook her head almost instantly. "No, Sir. I'd rather wait at home."

Manohar smiled, a reassuring warmth in his expression. "That's all right. Don't worry too much. I've seen how hard you've worked. You've given it your best, and that's what matters."

Simran glanced at him, her anxiety momentarily soothed by his calm confidence. There was something about the way he spoke—steady, sure, and unwavering—that always managed to put her at ease.

"I'll head to the school and check the results as soon as they're out," he added, his tone firm and reassuring.

As he walked away, Simran watched his retreating figure, her heart a curious mix of nervous anticipation and quiet hope. His confidence in her was contagious, even in small doses. For the first time in days, she allowed herself to believe that maybe—just maybe—things would turn out fine.

Chapter 15

RESULT DAY

Manohar arrived at Simran's school early that morning, but the grounds were already alive with a mix of students, parents, and teachers. The atmosphere buzzed with anticipation, the air thick with the kind of nervous energy that only comes before something monumental. Everywhere he looked, parents clutched their children's shoulders, offering silent reassurance, while students huddled in small groups, exchanging whispered comments and furtive glances.

Manohar carefully manoeuvred through the crowd, sidestepping clusters of excited teenagers and their families, his destination clear: the school office. As he moved forward, a familiar voice broke through the hum of the crowd.

"Sir, how are you?"

Manohar paused, recognising the speaker at once. It was Anjali, standing near the school gate with a few of her friends, her face lighting up when she saw him.

"I'm fine, Anjali. How are you?" Manohar replied with a nod, trying to keep his tone casual despite the anxious anticipation he felt for the task at hand.

Anjali's smile was wide, and she looked back at her friends before turning her attention back to him. "I'm doing well, Sir. But where's Simran? Why didn't you bring her along? It would have been nice to see her here with you."

A flicker of hesitation passed through Manohar's mind. He had known that Anjali often made casual remarks about Simran, teasing him in a playful, yet pointed way. Her tone suggested more than simple curiosity—she was always keen to understand the dynamics between him and his student.

"She's busy at home," Manohar said, trying to keep his tone light. "I came to collect her results."

Anjali's smile widened slightly, her eyes narrowing as though she had picked up on something unspoken in his words. "A tutor going out of his way for a student... you have high hopes for her, don't you, Sir?" she remarked with a teasing lilt in her voice.

Manohar met her gaze steadily, offering a smile that was both polite and measured. He knew this conversation held more weight than Anjali realised. "Simran has worked hard. I'm confident she'll do well. Good marks, for sure."

Anjali exchanged a knowing look with her friends, her smile lingering as if she understood the unspoken bond between them. "Of course," she said before turning away, her friends trailing behind her as they moved off towards the gate.

Manohar continued on his way to the school office, where the scene inside was as chaotic as he had imagined. Parents clustered around the counter, eagerly asking about their children's results, while clerks shuffled through a stack of papers. The noise of rising voices and the rustle of documents filled the room, a mixture of anticipation and the odd sigh of relief—or despair.

Manohar approached one of the clerks who glanced up from the stack of papers and offered a brief, distracted smile. "Can I help you?"

"I'm here for Simran Malhotra's results," Manohar said, raising his voice just enough to be heard over the clamour.

The clerk nodded, flipping through the pile before pulling out a sheet with Simran's name on it. "Simran Malhotra, Section B, right?" she asked, confirming the details.

Manohar nodded, his heart thudding in his chest as he watched her hand him the result. For a moment, everything around him seemed to fade away–the noise, the crowd, the chaos–until the only thing that existed was the piece of paper in his hands. He scanned the marks quickly, and a sense of satisfaction washed over him.

Simran had done it. She had not only passed, but she had exceeded expectations in a way that filled him with pride. Her results were a testament to the months of hard work, late nights, and tireless effort. And more than that, they were the culmination of their journey together, a journey that had started with confusion and frustration but ended in triumph.

A smile tugged at the corners of his lips as he carefully folded the paper and slipped it into his bag. As he did, a surge of excitement bubbled within him. He couldn't wait to share the news with Simran. She would be overjoyed.

The ride back to Simran's house felt quicker than usual, the bustling streets of the city blurring around him as he relished the moment. He was in a jolly mood, replaying the image of her result in his mind. He couldn't help but feel a quiet pride, not only for Simran's success but for his own role in helping her reach this point.

When the auto pulled up to her house, Manohar practically leapt out, eager to share the news. He rushed up to the door, his heart racing with anticipation.

"Simran, Simran!" he called out, his voice filled with excitement.

Simran, already waiting anxiously inside, hurried to the door. As she opened it, her wide eyes locked onto his, sensing the importance of what he was about to say.

"What happened, Sir?" she asked, her voice trembling with a mixture of hope and fear.

Manohar stepped inside, trying to hold back the excitement for just a moment longer. "Wait a second," he said, a grin spreading across his face as he looked at Simran and her mother. "Simran, my dream has come true!"

"Really, Sir?" Simran's voice quivered with anticipation, her heart hammering in her chest.

"You've done it," Manohar said, his voice thick with emotion. "You've got a first-class with 85 per cent marks, and in science, you've scored 90 per cent!"

Simran froze for a moment, her mind struggling to process the words. She stared at him, her eyes wide in disbelief, as though she couldn't quite grasp the magnitude of the moment. Mrs. Malhotra, who had been standing quietly in the background, began to weep softly, her tears a mix of pride, joy, and gratitude. She had never imagined such a result for her daughter.

"Simran, you did it!" Manohar said, his voice shaking, his pride in her evident.

Simran, her mind still reeling, finally let out a shaky breath, the reality of the moment slowly sinking in. The long hours of study, the late nights, the moments of doubt—everything had led to this. She had done it. And for Manohar, it wasn't just her success—it was the confirmation of what he had always known: that with enough dedication, anyone could overcome the odds. Today, Simran has proven that to both of them.

Simran sat motionless on the sofa, her mind struggling to comprehend the words she had just heard. The shock of the results seemed to echo through her body, making her legs tremble. Slowly, she stood up, as if her own body was unsure of how to respond to the flood of emotions that overtook her. With each step towards Manohar, the weight of the moment seemed to grow heavier, but her heart beat faster with every passing second. When she reached him, without a second thought, she threw her arms around him, clutching him as though he were the anchor in a storm. Her body shook with silent sobs.

"Sir, you're really great," she whispered between sobs, her voice trembling. "It's all because of you that I've become this sensible, this successful." Her words spilt out, raw and unrestrained, as if the dam had finally burst.

Manohar was taken aback, his heart constricting at the sight of Simran's tears. He gently patted her back, his own throat tight with emotion. "No, Simran," he said softly, his voice steady but warm. "It's your hard work and dedication that brought you here. I just showed you the path."

Simran pulled away slightly, looking up at him through tear-filled eyes as if trying to understand the truth in his words. It was as if, for the first time, she was beginning to realise that this success was not a gift, but something she had earned through her efforts. Manohar reached into his bag and pulled out the report card, handing it to her with a quiet smile.

Simran's hands trembled as she took the paper from him, almost afraid to look at it, as though seeing it might shatter the fragile reality of the moment. Slowly, her eyes scanned the marks but her mind struggled to catch up. The numbers seemed surreal, as though they belonged to someone else. She traced them with her fingers, each digit sinking in deeper until it felt like her heart was expanding with a mixture of pride and disbelief.

Tears welled up again, this time spilling down her cheeks freely. She looked back at Manohar, her voice barely audible, yet filled with emotion. "I couldn't have done this without you, Sir," she whispered, her words heavy with gratitude. "You believed in me when I didn't even believe in myself."

Manohar's heart swelled as he watched her, a quiet pride blooming inside him. It wasn't just the result he was proud of; it was the journey they had shared, the trust they had built over months of struggle. He smiled, his gaze soft and reassuring. "The future is yours now, Simran. Keep going, and never doubt what you're capable of."

In that moment, as they stood together, surrounded by the warmth of her mother's pride and the quiet strength of their bond, Simran felt something shift within her. The uncertainty that had once clouded her path began to clear. For the first time, she believed—truly believed—that she had the power to shape her own destiny. It wasn't just about the marks on the paper or the approval of others. It was about her own belief in herself, the belief that had been rekindled by the unwavering faith of the man standing beside her.

Chapter 16

ECHOES OF GOODBYE

Manohar's visit to Simran's house after her admission process at Delhi University began with the usual warmth. They exchanged pleasantries as she told him how everything was falling into place, how her future was beginning to take shape. But as the conversation went on, something in the air shifted–a subtle change that Simran couldn't quite put her finger on.

"Simran, you have a bright future," Manohar said, his voice full of pride, his eyes shining with hope for her future.

Simran, always trusting in his words, looked up at him with a soft smile. "I can try my best, Sir, but if you guide me properly, I know I can achieve anything."

His smile faltered slightly, and he leaned back, the pride in his voice giving way to something deeper, something heavier. "It's true, Simran. But now you have to choose your career." There was an almost distant tone to his words, a shift that made Simran pause. She hadn't missed it, and she sensed that this moment, though seemingly casual, was about to change everything.

After a brief silence, Manohar cleared his throat. "Can you give me a glass of water, please?" His voice, though polite, seemed strained as if he were carefully choosing his words.

Simran, not yet aware of what was coming, stood up and walked towards the fridge. As she fetched a bottle of water and poured it into a glass, she glanced back at him. He was sitting still, his face turned downward, deep in thought. His usual calm appearance seemed shattered by something unseen. She could feel a heaviness in the air, thick with unsaid words.

"Sir, are you okay?" Simran asked, walking back towards him, concern evident in her voice. "You look... puzzled."

Manohar didn't immediately respond. He stared ahead, his eyes distant, lost in a thought that seemed far too heavy to bear. The ticking of the clock in the corner of the room sounded louder, more pronounced. It was 4:30 pm. The sunlight poured through the windows, casting long shadows across the room, but the warmth of the light did nothing to ease the chill that had settled between them.

Taking a deep breath, Manohar spoke, his voice quieter now, as though he were confiding in her. "Simran, it seems... my marriage is fixed."

The words hit Simran like a sharp gust of wind, freezing her in place. She stood motionless, the glass in her hand forgotten. The room seemed to close in around her, the space growing smaller with every passing second. "What are you saying, Sir?" she managed to ask, her voice small, her heart pounding hard now.

Manohar's gaze dropped to the floor, his hands clasped together as if to steady himself. "Yesterday, I received a letter from my grandfather. He mentioned a family back home...

and they've found a girl for me. He asked me to accept their choice."

Simran felt the room tilt as her mind struggled to process what he had just said. It felt like the ground had been swept from beneath her. "When will you meet her?" she asked, her voice trembling, a quiet fear settling over her.

"In our tradition," Manohar said, his words steady but carrying a resigned finality, "we don't meet before marriage. It's decided by the family."

Simran's heart dropped. She couldn't make sense of what he was saying. "But... Sir, how can you marry someone you've never even met?" The words escaped before she could stop them, a mixture of disbelief and confusion in her voice.

Manohar gave a faint smile, a sad, knowing smile, but it did nothing to ease the ache in Simran's chest. "It's how things work in our society. The girl's family background is more important than meeting her in person."

Simran's thoughts raced, her emotions swirling like a storm. How could this be happening? She had always admired Manohar for his progressive thinking, for the way he'd always stood for fairness and reason. How could he, someone she had come to trust so deeply, surrender to such outdated traditions? "Do you even know what she looks like? Or anything about her?" she asked, her voice barely above a whisper as if pleading for him to offer some small detail that could make sense of it all.

"No, Simran," Manohar replied softly, his voice distant, "I haven't seen her picture yet. We don't usually ask for photographs before marriage. But I'm sure my family has made the right decision."

Simran's world seemed to unravel. The idea of him marrying someone without even knowing her, without any love between them, was impossible to grasp. The very core of her beliefs, the values that had held her up through the darkest times, now felt fragile and shaken. She couldn't understand how the man who had once inspired her to follow her path could be trapped in this web of tradition. "Without knowing each other, you're supposed to become life partners?" she asked, her voice breaking under the weight of her emotions.

The silence that followed was thick, suffocating. Simran felt as though the walls were closing in on her, and in that silence, the ticking of the clock became deafening. Manohar could see the pain in her eyes, but he felt powerless to change the path he had been set upon. The anguish was visible in every line of his face, but he couldn't escape it.

Sensing that he had said all he could, he stood up slowly, his movements deliberate, as if every step carried a burden he couldn't bear. "Can I go, Simran?" His voice was soft, almost apologetic.

Simran barely heard him; her mind was still reeling from the shock. She nodded slowly, her heart sinking with each movement he made. "Yes, Sir, you can go," she whispered, the words feeling hollow as they left her lips.

As Manohar turned and walked towards the door, Simran felt the sharp pang of loss. She watched him leave, her heart heavy with the unspoken words that hung between them. With the click of the door behind him, the silence in the room became unbearable, the ticking of the clock now sounding like the echo of her shattered dreams.

She sat there alone, her eyes vacant and her hands trembling. The room that had once felt like a place of warmth and promise now felt like a cage, the weight of the future pressing down on her shoulders.

Chapter 17

BONTA PARK

Simran had spent the days after Manohar's visit in quiet turmoil. Her thoughts tangled between the deep ache of his decision and the weight of her own emotions. At first, the blow had left her shattered, breaking her heart into pieces. She had considered confiding in her parents, perhaps even ending her life altogether. But time, as it often does, had changed her. The fragile, naive girl who had once looked up to him with only admiration had grown stronger, more resolute. The pain had not faded, but it had turned into a force that pushed her forward. Manohar's influence on her had been profound. He had taught her to question, to think critically, to stand on her own. And now, she was no longer the same Simran. She was ready to face him—not as a lost girl, but as a woman who knew what she wanted and what she could no longer accept.

It was clear to her now that she needed to make him see, make him understand. Love, real love, had to transcend the confines of caste and tradition. There could be no place for these archaic beliefs in their future. If there was a place to confront him, it would be here—Bonta Park. This quiet sanctuary, nestled in the northern part of Old Delhi, had always been a refuge for Simran. A serene escape from the world's noise, it was a place that spoke to the heart. With its endless trails, the shade of old trees and the occasional glimpse of history in the form of the Mutiny Memorial and Flagstaff Tower, it had always been a place of reflection. The park felt like a world unto itself—away from the suffocating expectations, the rules that dictated so much of their lives.

As Simran stood at the edge of the park, she made a silent promise to herself. She would change his mind. She would make him see that tradition could not stand in the way of love.

The next day, they met in the park. The sun was gentle, filtering through the trees and casting soft patterns of light and shadow. The air was thick with the scent of blooming flowers, and the quiet was punctuated only by the occasional chirp of a bird or the rustle of leaves in the wind. They walked side by side, but Simran could feel the weight of her thoughts pulling at her, a heavy burden she was determined to share.

They eventually found a bench beneath a large bougainvillaea, its brilliant pink flowers fluttering to the ground like confetti. Simran took a deep breath, her resolve hardening. This was it. There was no turning back now.

"Sir," she began, her voice steady but tinged with emotion, "do you ever wonder why things never change?"

Manohar, sensing something was amiss, looked at her with a confused expression. "What do you mean, Simran?"

She turned to him, her eyes searching his face as if trying to find the right words. "You came to Delhi for a brighter future, for a better career. You're so intelligent, so well-read. You've taught me to question everything—to challenge what we're told. But when it comes to your own life, why are you still bound by these old traditions? Why haven't you become more modern, more free in your thinking?"

Manohar's eyes dropped, a sigh escaping him. "It's not that simple. Tradition is part of who we are, part of our identity. My family has always followed these customs. It's what they expect and my grandfather has made it clear—he wants me to marry within our caste. It's a decision made for me, and I've learned to accept that."

Simran's frustration bubbled to the surface. "But don't you see, Sir? You've taught me to think beyond what's expected of me and to question the rules. You made me believe that I could be more than just what society tells me to be. Why can't you do the same for yourself? Why let these old customs dictate your life?"

Manohar's gaze shifted away as if her words were piercing into him, but he couldn't find the strength to answer. This wasn't the same Manohar she had known—a man who had shown her the world beyond the narrow walls of tradition. This was a man trapped by the expectations of his family, a man torn between duty and desire.

"I don't know, Simran," he said finally, his voice low, almost resigned. "Maybe it's easier this way. Easier to follow what's been laid out for me than to fight against it. My family's wishes… they're hard to go against."

Simran shook her head, disbelief flooding her chest. "But what about what you want, Sir? What about your happiness? Are you really okay with marrying someone you don't even know—just because tradition says you should? Is that the future you want?"

The words hung in the air, charged with emotion, as Manohar's thoughts raced. For the first time, he felt torn. It was as if the world he had grown up in was no longer enough to sustain him. He had taught Simran to be bold, to follow her path. But now, here she was, asking him to do the very thing he had urged her to do–to be brave enough to live a life of his own choosing.

Simran softened her tone, trying to make him understand. "I'm not saying that tradition doesn't have its place, Sir. But should it come at the expense of your happiness? Should it stop you from choosing the life you truly want? The life you've always taught me to fight for?"

Manohar's eyes locked with hers, his expression a mix of confusion and realisation. "You're right, Simran. I've always encouraged you to be independent, to chase your dreams, and yet, I've never allowed myself to do the same. I've let tradition control me."

Simran smiled gently, though it was tinged with sadness. "Sir, you have so much potential. You've shown me that the world is bigger than the boxes society puts us in. Don't you deserve to live by the same principles you've taught me? You don't have to accept a future decided for you."

Manohar sat back, the weight of her words pressing down on him. The silence between them was not uncomfortable, but filled with an understanding that had not been there before. He was beginning to see that his choices—his submission to tradition—had never been as free as he had believed.

"I don't know if I can change everything all at once," he said slowly, his voice filled with uncertainty but also a quiet determination. "But maybe... maybe I can start with this. Maybe I can take that first step."

Simran's eyes sparkled with hope. "You don't have to change everything, Sir. Just take one step. One small step towards the life you want."

They sat in silence, the rustling of the leaves in the breeze offering a gentle soundtrack to the moment. The park, so calm and quiet, seemed to echo the shift taking place within Manohar.

"Thank you, Simran," he said finally, his voice sincere and soft. "You've made me see things in a different way."

Simran smiled, a warmth spreading through her chest. "I didn't do anything, Sir. You've always had the answers. You just needed someone to help you see them."

As they sat there, watching the sun dip lower in the sky, casting a golden glow over the park, both of them felt a sense of peace, a quiet understanding between them. It was as if the future had unfolded just a little bit more clearly, and for the first time, Manohar felt the courage to choose for himself.

The park, with its lush greenery and quiet beauty, had become a symbol of the choice he now had to make.

Tradition or love? Duty or happiness? The world he had always known, or the one Simran had opened his eyes to?

Manohar knew that the path ahead would not be easy. But for the first time, he felt ready to take the first step. And with that, something deep inside him began to shift.

As the evening light faded and the park grew quieter, Simran's heart held a quiet hope. She had given him the courage to see beyond his limitations. Now, it was up to him to find the strength to live the life he had always deserved.

Chapter 18

UPSC EXAM

For the past four years, Manohar had lived and breathed the UPSC exams. Each day, he submerged himself in textbooks, practice papers and mock interviews, the hours stretching endlessly, often with little to show for it. His first attempt had been a crushing blow—he had not even cleared the preliminary round. Yet, as each year passed, his resolve had only strengthened. He managed to clear the prelims in his next few attempts, only to falter in the Mains. In the MPPSC (Madhya Pradesh Public Service Commission) exam, he made it to the final stage—the interview—but even then, the elusive victory slipped through his fingers.

Now, he stood at the threshold of his final UPSC attempt. The pressure was immense. If this attempt failed, he knew he would have to walk away from his dream of the civil services and chart a new course. The thought worried him, the uncertainty looming large. But even as he contemplated this, his passion for writing, which had first taken root in his teenage years, quietly called to him. His articles had appeared in local newspapers and journals, and every publication, every piece of feedback from his readers, gave him a sense of purpose he couldn't ignore. The world of journalism, the field he had nearly pursued instead of the administrative services, beckoned once again. If UPSC slipped through his fingers, perhaps this was where his future lay. But that thought seemed almost like a resignation. Writing, though fulfilling, wasn't as stable or as respected as the life he had imagined in the civil services.

Manohar's mind buzzed as he got up early one crisp morning. The weak light of dawn filtered in through the curtains, the soft sounds of the waking city drifting in from the street below. He stretched, feeling the familiar tightness in his muscles from long nights spent hunched over books. The air was cool and refreshing, a stark contrast to the heaviness that weighed on him.

He quickly washed up and made his way to the small wooden desk he had set up in his room, papers scattered around like a battlefield, highlighters and pens strewn across the surface. The faint smell of tea rose from the kitchen, where his roommate was already at work, preparing breakfast. The rhythm of their mornings had become a comforting routine, the silence broken only by the sounds of study and the occasional comment about an upcoming test or a recent lecture.

Manohar opened his first book of the day–a guide on Indian polity–and settled into the rhythm of study. His eyes skimmed over the words, the concepts of governance and constitutional amendments stirring memories of countless hours spent in the same position. His notebook, already half-full with scrawled notes and underlined phrases, was evidence of his efforts. The familiar rush of anxiety mixed with determination surged through him as he began writing down key points. Every fact, every detail, was a step closer to his goal.

"Manohar, breakfast is ready!" his roommate's voice broke through his concentration.

"Coming!" he called back, reluctantly closing the book. Breakfast was a welcome break–a time to recharge and connect with someone who shared his struggle. The conversation at the table was casual, the focus on the day's study plan and the mock tests they would tackle together. Despite the pressure they both faced, there was an unspoken companionship, a shared understanding of what it meant to chase an elusive dream.

After they finished breakfast, Manohar returned to his desk, where the sunlight had now fully taken over, filling the small room with warmth. He began revising previous years' papers, his eyes scanning the questions, marking the ones that posed the greatest challenge. The minutes ticked by, and the pressure of the exam seemed to mount with each passing second.

But then, like a fleeting shadow, his thoughts drifted to Simran. The conversation they had shared at Bonta Park played in his mind on a loop. Her words, so full of passion and resolve, had struck a chord deep within him. Simran, the girl who had come to him for guidance, had somehow become a mirror, reflecting to him the questions he had been avoiding for years. She wasn't just a student anymore; she had become a force, challenging him to rethink everything—his views on tradition, on love, and on his own life.

He paused, his pen poised over the paper, as her voice echoed in his mind. He was studying for an exam, yes, but somewhere along the way, his personal life had started to bleed into his studies. Simran had made him confront not only the vast ocean of knowledge that awaited him in the world of governance but also the deep, uncharted waters of his own heart. The dilemma between his duty and his desires, between love and tradition, had become impossible to ignore.

With a sigh, Manohar resumed his studies, trying to push aside the thoughts that had nothing to do with constitutional law or the intricacies of public administration. But even as he flipped through the pages, his mind kept returning to the conversation with Simran—her questions about tradition, about the life he had built for himself and the life he truly wanted to lead. Could he continue to live in the shadow of expectations? Or was it time to step into the light of his own desires, to forge a path that was truly his?

The day wore on, and Manohar found himself caught in a swirl of conflicting thoughts. His resolve to prepare for the UPSC exam was strong, but so were the questions Simran had planted in his heart. He knew the exam was just around the corner, but the real test was not going to be on paper—it would be the choice he would have to make between the life he had always known and the life he could create.

As the hours passed and the sun dipped lower in the sky, Manohar felt the weight of his decisions more keenly than ever. Whether he succeeded in the UPSC exam or not, one thing was clear: his journey was far from over, and the road ahead would be shaped not just by his intellect, but by his heart as well.

Chapter 19

PASS OR FAIL?

Today was the day–the day that held the power to transform everything. Manohar rose with the early light, his mind already whirling with thoughts of the UPSC Mains result, which was due to be announced by noon. The familiar weight of uncertainty pressed on his chest, but he moved through his morning routine almost mechanically, his mind too busy to linger on any one thought for long. He slipped into his usual crisp shirt and worn trousers, the fabric slightly frayed from months of use, and rushed out of his room, his heart hammering with each hurried step.

At the bus stop, Manohar checked his watch for the umpteenth time. His breath came in shallow bursts, a mixture of anxiety and anticipation flooding his senses. He boarded the familiar DTC Route No. 26, which would take him directly to Dholpur House, the imposing UPSC office near India Gate. As the bus lurched into motion, the chaotic streets of Delhi unfolded outside the window. The familiar hum of city life—the honking horns, the clatter of rickshaws, the busy crowds—was drowned out by the rapid beating of his heart. He gripped the metal rail above his head, knuckles whitening with tension, while his eyes darted to the passing landmarks. They seemed distant today, as though the weight of his hopes and fears had blurred the cityscape into an unrecognisable haze.

The journey stretched on for what seemed like hours, though it was only about an hour before the bus finally pulled to a stop. Manohar stepped off, his shoes rattling against the pavement as he took in the sight of the grand colonial buildings surrounding him. The atmosphere felt heavier now, the significance of the moment settling in his bones. His feet carried him quickly through the busy street, but his mind was adrift, lost in a sea of doubt and hope. He reached the iron gate of the UPSC office, his eyes scanning the scene, only to feel a sudden jolt of disappointment. The gate was locked.

"The result will be displayed on the notice board after an hour," the security guard said, his tone indifferent.

One hour. A long, torturous hour. Manohar nodded numbly and turned away, his mind whirling with anxious thoughts. He tried to distract himself by walking around, but every step only seemed to deepen the sense of unease. What if he passed? What if he failed? The possibilities clashed violently in his mind. The idea of success ignited a flicker of excitement, but the thought of failure—of all those years of effort culminating in nothing—made his stomach twist.

As if on autopilot, he found himself standing in front of a popular *chaat* house, the mouth-watering smell of spices and fried snacks tempting him into the queue. It was a small distraction, a fleeting moment of comfort amidst the chaos in his mind. The tangy, spicy flavours of the *chaat* briefly soothed him, the crispy *papdi* crunching between his teeth, the sweetness of tamarind chutney offering a brief escape from the uncertainty. But as soon as the plate was empty, reality returned, the clock ticking relentlessly towards the result.

Half an hour later, Manohar returned to the UPSC office. This time, the gate was open. A large crowd had gathered around the notice board, their eyes fixed on the list of roll numbers. Manohar's heart pounded as he pushed his way through the throng, his legs unsteady but determined. The atmosphere was thick with tension—some faces bright with joy, others grim with dread. There were hugs and cheers from those who had passed, tears of happiness streaking down their faces. But the majority of the crowd stood still, staring at the board, their expressions hollow and defeated.

Manohar's pulse quickened. He squeezed his way to the front, his eyes scanning the list of roll numbers. He scanned quickly, his breath shallow, his hands trembling. He looked from top to bottom, hoping, praying that somehow his roll number would appear. But it wasn't there. His heart skipped a beat. He tried again, this time starting from the bottom, convinced he had missed it. But the numbers blurred together, his mind refusing to process the reality in front of him.

His roll number wasn't there. It was gone. It was over.

The world around him seemed to collapse in slow motion. The cheers, the sobs, the shuffling of feet—all faded into the background. Manohar took a step back, his head spinning, and the coldness of failure creeping up on him. His dreams of becoming an administrative officer, all the long hours of study, the sacrifices—everything had led to this single moment and now it had slipped through his fingers.

He stood there for a few moments, staring blankly at the noticeboard. His mind felt empty, a void where his thoughts should have been. This was the end of the road, the culmination of a journey that had started with such hope. The victory he had imagined—seeing his roll number posted proudly on the board, the sense of accomplishment—was nowhere to be found. Instead, all he felt was a crushing silence, an emptiness that pressed on him from all sides.

As he turned to leave, his thoughts drifted to Simran, to everything that had unfolded between them. She had always believed in him, always held him in such high regard. And now, he had failed—not just himself, but her as well. The weight of that realisation hit him harder than anything else. Manohar's feet felt heavy as he made his way back to the bus stop, his heart dragging with him. The path he had set out on had come to a sudden halt, and he had no choice but to find a new way forward. The journey he had envisioned for so long was over. What came next, he didn't know—but he would have to figure it out, one step at a time.

Chapter 20

SHIFT IN PATH

Manohar walked back to his flat, each step heavier than the last. The world around him seemed dimmer, his thoughts weighed down by the crushing sense of defeat. When he finally reached the door, he didn't even bother to say a word to his flatmates. Without a glance in their direction, he went straight to his room, closed the door, and collapsed onto his bed. His body felt like it had been drained of all energy, his mind racing through the events of the day—the unbearable moments at the UPSC office, the hope and dread that had twisted inside him, and the harsh reality that now lay in front of him. His dreams, once vivid and alive, now felt irreparably shattered.

As he lay there, staring blankly at the ceiling, the past came rushing back to him, flooding his thoughts. He remembered the day he had left Darbhanga, the small town that had always been home. His family had not been able to support him financially, yet he had promised them, "Whatever you can send, I will manage. I will never ask for more." And true to his word, he hadn't. Despite the hardships he had faced in Delhi, he had never once asked for anything beyond what they could provide. He had learned to survive on the bare minimum, sacrificing comfort in the pursuit of his dream.

His father's voice echoed in his mind, a reminder of all the sacrifices made. "I can support you until 1995; after that, it will be difficult," his father had said, knowing that his own retirement was fast approaching. The weight of that statement pressed heavily on Manohar's chest now. He had one more chance to crack the UPSC, but how long could he keep fighting this battle? His father's words were a constant reminder of the fleeting nature of time. It felt like the clock was ticking down, and with each passing day, he was running out of options.

That night, sleep escaped him. Manohar lay in the darkness, unable to escape the turmoil in his mind. Regret, fear, and sadness swirled inside him. His thoughts wandered back to Darbhanga, to the family that had pinned their hopes on him, to the sacrifices they had made so that he could have a chance at something more. He had been their pride, their hope for a better future. But now, it felt as though he had let them all down. The failure stung more deeply than he had anticipated. It wasn't just his own dreams that had been shattered—it was theirs too.

The next morning, despite the exhaustion that weighed him down, Manohar made a decision. He stood up, pulled himself together, and left the flat. The cool morning air didn't do much to ease the tension that gripped his chest, but he moved forward with determination. He walked to Bharatiya Vidya Bhavan, a well-known institute in Delhi, and purchased the application forms for journalism and mass communication. It felt almost surreal. For years, he had poured his heart and soul into the civil services, and now he was choosing a different path—one that had always intrigued him but that he had never fully embraced.

As he walked back to the flat, the weight of the decision settled on him. It felt like a pivot, a major turning point in his life. This wasn't the path he had envisioned, but it felt right in a way that the UPSC journey no longer did. He had always loved writing, ever since his school days, and now he was finally going to pursue that passion. There was a sense of relief, but also an undercurrent of doubt. Was he really making the right choice?

When he entered the flat, his flatmates immediately noticed the shift in his demeanour. There was a quiet tension in the air, a question hanging unasked.

"Hey Manohar, don't lose heart!" one of them said, trying to offer a few words of encouragement. "You still have one attempt left for UPSC. I'm sure you'll make it next time!"

Manohar shook his head slowly, a small, sad smile playing on his lips. "I'm sorry," he said softly, his voice carrying the weight of the night before. "I don't have the patience for another attempt. I've decided to take admission in journalism."

His flatmate blinked, clearly taken aback. "What? You're just going to give up? After all the years you've spent on this?"

Manohar sighed deeply, his eyes reveal the sleepless nights and the emotional turmoil that had gripped him. "It's not about giving up," he said, his voice quiet but firm.

"I've realised that UPSC isn't my path anymore. I've always loved writing. It's been my passion since school. UPSC was a dream, yes, but it's not my only dream."

His flatmate tried to protest, but Manohar's resolve was clear. His voice was calm, though tinged with sorrow. "I can't live with this uncertainty anymore. My father is retiring next year, and I can't keep depending on them. I need to start earning, and journalism feels like the right move for me."

That evening, the reality of his decision began to set in. He walked to his desk, gathered his UPSC notes and study materials, and began to pack them up. One by one, he handed them over to his flatmates—many of whom were still chasing the dream he had just let go of. There was a quiet solemnity in the room as they watched him give away the books that had once been his constant companions during countless late-night study sessions.

As Manohar handed over the last book, a sense of finality hung in the air. His journey with UPSC had ended, but something new was beginning. It wasn't easy—letting go of a dream he had held onto for so long. But there was a quiet hope in the air too, a feeling that this wasn't the end, but the start of something different, something that felt more aligned with who he was.

That night, Manohar closed the door to his room with a sense of relief. The burden of UPSC, the pressure of expectations, was finally lifted. He had taken his first step towards a new chapter in his life—a chapter where he could pursue his true passion. As he lay down in bed, sleep finally came to him, deep and peaceful, the storm of the past few days giving way to a much-needed calm.

Chapter 21

SWIRL OF THOUGHTS

Simran stood frozen for a moment, the news about Manohar's UPSC result reverberating in her mind like an unexpected shock. A whirlwind of thoughts swirled inside her. Could it have been because of all the time he spent tutoring me? Could my studies have distracted him? No, no—she quickly corrected herself. Sir was always so practical, so disciplined. He would never have let something like that derail his career. Maybe it was simply because he needed the money and tutoring was more of a necessity than a choice.

Yet, despite her logical reasoning, a seed of doubt began to take root. Did I unknowingly become a distraction for him? She wondered. Maybe all those late-night sessions, the hours spent helping her with her studies, had cost him precious time he could have spent focusing on his own future. The guilt began to aggravate her, even though she knew deep down that Manohar had always been dedicated, always so professional. Still, the thought lingered. She tried to shake it off. No, sir wouldn't let anything affect his career. He's always been so focused, so clear-headed... But the doubt remained, quietly tugging at her conscience.

It wasn't long before Manohar arrived at Simran's house, his face a picture of calm resignation. He had clearly accepted what had happened, but the weight of his disappointment still hung heavily in the air. As they settled into the familiar comfort of her home, he broke the news that he had made a decision. He was giving up on his civil services dream and pursuing a career in journalism.

"Sir, that's a very good field," Simran said, her voice laced with gentle optimism, trying to lift his spirits.

"Every field has its value," Manohar replied, though his tone carried a hint of frustration. "But it's not the same as IAS or IPS. If I had joined journalism four years ago, I'd probably be settled in Delhi by now, working for a leading newspaper or magazine. But who can predict destiny, right?"

Simran watched as a brief flash of regret passed through his eyes. "I'm four years behind," he added, his voice tinged with quiet bitterness. It was as if the weight of all his failed attempts had suddenly grown heavier at that moment.

"No, Sir!" Simran insisted, determined to pull him back from that dark place. "You still have time to achieve your goals. This is a new path, and with your knowledge and writing skills, you'll thrive in journalism. Don't let this setback define you."

Her words seemed to soften the edges of his frustration, and for the next half hour, they continued their conversation. They discussed journalism—its potential, the opportunities it offered, and how Manohar's passion for writing could now be channelled into something new and fulfilling. His mood lightened, though the shadows of doubt still lingered in his eyes.

Then, with a small but bright smile, Simran shared her good news. "Sir, I got into a prestigious college at Delhi University," she announced, her excitement contagious.

Manohar's face immediately brightened. "Really? You got in?" he asked, his surprise evident.

"Yes, Sir," she said, her smile widening. "And it's all thanks to your guidance. Without you, I wouldn't have made it this far."

Manohar's eyes gleamed with pride and happiness. "That's incredible news, Simran. You've succeeded where I—"

But before he could finish his thought, Simran gently interrupted. "No, Sir. You've succeeded too, in your own way. You've inspired me. Now, you're following your passion. Journalism may not have the same prestige as IAS or IPS, but it has its own bright side. You have the power to influence and inform the world through your words."

Manohar listened intently as Simran spoke, her words filled with wisdom and grace beyond her years. Her confidence and maturity seemed to pour into him, soothing the self-doubt that had started to settle like a weight in his chest. She reminded him of the pivotal role he had played in her life and how his guidance had shaped her future.

"You've given me the tools to succeed, Sir," she continued, her voice steady. "Now it's time for you to find success in your path."

Manohar smiled, feeling something stir within him—a renewed sense of purpose. Simran's optimism was like a light breaking through the fog of uncertainty. Her words began to chase away the lingering shadows of doubt, and he realised that life wasn't a straight line. Just because his original dream hadn't come to fruition didn't mean there wasn't another path waiting for him. A new chapter was beginning, one that might not have been the one he had planned, but one that held its own promise and potential.

And for the first time in days, Manohar felt hopeful.

Chapter 22

AMIT & PRITA

Manohar's life at Bhartiya Vidya Bhavan had brought with it a refreshing new perspective. Every afternoon, he would leave his flat around 3:30 p.m., catching the familiar DTC bus that would take him from his colony to Kasturba Gandhi Marg. It was a daily routine that had grown comforting, offering him a few quiet moments to think as he arrived early enough to soak in the campus atmosphere before his classes began. The institute was alive with energy, its air filled with the hum of passionate discussions on current affairs, media ethics, and the ever-evolving world of journalism.

His classes, which began at 5 p.m. sharp, were dynamic and engaging, with faculty who brought years of experience to the table. The students, like him, were driven—eager to carve out a name for themselves in the world of words. Among them, Manohar had forged a close friendship with Amit, a fellow student from his nearby colony in Kamla Nagar. Amit was sharp, intelligent, and highly educated, coming from a financially well-off family. Despite his privileged background, he was grounded, humble, and soft-spoken. It didn't take long for the two to become fast friends, bonding over shared interests in journalism, media trends, and life in general. Their friendship flourished as they rode the crowded DTC buses together, debating the latest news stories and critiquing the coverage they saw in newspapers.

Amit was someone Manohar deeply admired—not only for his sharp wit and intelligence but also for his resourcefulness. Their discussions often delved into the finer aspects of journalism, from media strategies to the best investigative reporting. Their minds seemed to mesh seamlessly, and they could easily lose track of time, caught up in their passionate conversations.

One evening, as Manohar arrived at the campus early, he spotted Amit in the cafeteria. He was deep in conversation with a girl. Manohar didn't recognise her. She was also enrolled in the same journalism course, but this was the first time Manohar had seen her. What caught his attention, however, wasn't just the girl's unfamiliar face—it was the way Amit was talking to her. He'd always imagined Amit as someone who would be drawn to a polished, sophisticated woman. This girl, though, didn't fit that image at all.

She was dark-skinned, dressed in simple, unremarkable clothes, and her appearance seemed almost carelessly put together. By society's standards, she didn't fit the kind of girl Amit would be interested in. Yet, despite her plain looks, there was something about her that intrigued Manohar— her voice. It was deep, rich, and captivating, almost like a radio jockey's smooth, confident tone. If one were to close their eyes, they might imagine her to be someone glamorous, someone who would stand out in any crowd.

Curious, Manohar found himself observing them more closely. He noticed how effortlessly they laughed together, how easy it seemed for Amit to open up in her presence. There was a comfort in the way they interacted, a subtle connection that suggested their bond was more than just friendly. Amit, usually reserved and polite with others, was expressive and at ease with her. The way he spoke to her— more open, more unguarded—was different from how he interacted with anyone else.

At first, Manohar struggled to reconcile this image of Amit with his understanding of him. How could someone as particular, as polished, as Amit be so drawn to someone who seemed so far removed from his world? But as the days went by and he continued to watch them interact, a realisation began to take shape in Manohar's mind: they were in love.

It didn't matter that she didn't meet society's standards of beauty or that her background wasn't anything like Amit's. What mattered was the connection they shared, one that transcended appearances and expectations. This revelation left Manohar with a lingering thought: Was love really about appearance? Or was it something deeper, something that couldn't be captured by outward appearances or superficial judgements?

Manohar didn't pry into Amit's private life–he respected his friend's boundaries–but he couldn't help but feel a sense of admiration for the bond between Amit and the girl. He understood now that love often defied societal norms and crossed boundaries of appearance, class, and background. It wasn't always about what the world expected; it was about what two people found in each other, regardless of how the world might judge them.

This realisation began to shape Manohar's evolving views on relationships, self-perception, and societal expectations. He found himself reflecting on his ideas about love—how often, it seemed, those ideas were influenced by external pressures rather than the true nature of connection.

But the curiosity about Amit and his relationship with this girl—who, as he soon learned, was named Prita—kept gnawing at Manohar's mind. How could someone like Amit, so focused on his future and so particular about everything, fall for someone who didn't seem to fit the image of his ideal partner? It confused him. Amit had always struck him as logical, sharp, and driven. And yet, here he was, seemingly involved with someone completely outside the world Manohar had imagined for him.

✳ ✳ ✳

One evening, as Manohar and Amit walked back from their journalism class, the warm glow of the setting sun bathed the streets in hues of amber. Their conversations usually meandered through light-hearted topics, but that day, Manohar felt a pull to address something deeper.

"Amit, how's life treating you these days?" Manohar asked, his tone casual, yet with an undertone of curiosity.

Amit glanced at him with a smile, his usual easy-going demeanour evident. "Same old routine—classes, assignments and prepping for projects. Nothing new."

Manohar chuckled, letting the conversation flow before steering it towards his real question. "And the faculty? Still tolerable?"

"They're fine. Though, honestly, some could use a crash course in enthusiasm," Amit joked, mimicking a particularly monotone professor. Their laughter echoed in the stillness of the evening.

It was the perfect moment to broach the subject that had been weighing on Manohar's mind. He cleared his throat. "Amit, there's something I've noticed lately… something I've been curious about."

Amit arched an eyebrow. "Curious? About what?"

"I've seen you at the cafeteria, often with a girl. Who is she?" Manohar tried to sound nonchalant, though his question carried genuine interest.

"Oh, you mean Prita?" Amit said with a short laugh. "She's just a friend."

"Just a friend?" Manohar's grin widened, his tone teasing. "Come on, Amit. I've seen how you two look at each other. There's more to it, isn't there?"

Amit hesitated for a moment, then sighed. "Okay, fine. Yes, we are more than friends. But it's not as simple as you think."

"Not simple?" Manohar asked, leaning in slightly. "What's complicated about it?"

Amit looked ahead, his expression pensive. "She's not from a privileged background. Her family struggles financially, and she doesn't fit the 'ideal' match people expect for me. But she's remarkable. She's talented, driven, and one of the most self-reliant people I've ever met."

Manohar frowned, trying to reconcile Amit's words with his own ingrained beliefs. "But… she doesn't match you in terms of family, looks, or, you know… caste?"

Amit stopped and turned to face him, his gaze steady. "Manohar, is that what matters to you? Looks, caste, and status? Let me ask you something. Have you ever tuned into Times FM in the morning?"

"Sure," Manohar replied, slightly thrown by the sudden shift. "I love their 'Good Morning Delhi' programme. The RJ has such an incredible voice—so vibrant and relatable."

"That RJ," Amit said, his smile softening, "is Prita."

Manohar stopped in his tracks, stunned. "What? The same Prita? She's the one behind that voice?"

"Yes," Amit said, a hint of pride in his voice. "She's made a name for herself despite her background. That's what I admire about her—the way she's built her life with grit and determination."

Manohar was silent for a moment, the revelation leaving him awestruck. He had imagined someone polished and glamorous behind that voice, not the simple, unassuming girl he'd seen with Amit.

"But Amit," he ventured cautiously, "what about your family? You know how traditional they are. How will they react?"

"They'll object, no doubt," Amit admitted, his tone firm. "They'll want someone from our caste and social standing. But I can't let those expectations dictate my life. Prita is more than her background. She's my choice, and I'm ready to stand by it."

Manohar felt a surge of admiration for his friend. Amit's resolve was unwavering even in the face of societal and familial pressures. For Manohar, whose own life was an ongoing tug-of-war between tradition and personal desires, Amit's clarity was both inspiring and unsettling.

As they reached their stop, the weight of the conversation lingered. Manohar returned to his flat that night, his mind abuzz with conflicting thoughts. He lay awake, staring at the ceiling, questioning his own hesitations. If Amit, with all his privileges and responsibilities, could take a stand, why couldn't he?

❄ ❄ ❄

The next morning, Manohar couldn't shake the need for clarity. Amit's words from the previous day lingered in his mind like an unanswered question. It was Sunday, and he knew Amit would be at his flat in Kamla Nagar—a lively hub near Delhi University's North Campus. The neighbourhood was a kaleidoscope of energy: narrow streets bustling with students, shoppers, and street vendors. Shops selling books, trendy clothes, and spicy street food lined the lanes, their displays vying for attention. The air was a symphony of honking rickshaws, laughter, and the sizzling of *aloo tikki* on hot skillets.

One of the most striking features of Kamla Nagar is its vibrant connection to the University of Delhi. The market, bustling with energy, often doubles as an informal fashion runway for college students. Young men and women, dressed in the latest trends, stroll through its lanes, effortlessly blending the charm of youth with contemporary style. For those who frequent the area, it's an unspoken truth–if you're looking to catch a glimpse of the best-dressed crowd in Delhi, Kamla Nagar is the place to be.

Its proximity to the university ensures a constant flow of students, especially in the evenings when the market comes alive. The chatter of friends, the laughter over shared snacks, and the occasional debate about the latest movies or campus events fill the air. Among the boys, there's a running joke that has become almost legendary: "If you want to see the most beautiful girls in Delhi, just take a walk through Kamla Nagar market." It's said with a mix of humour and admiration, capturing the spirit of a place where youth, style, and life converge.

But Kamla Nagar is more than just a hotspot for fashionable students. It's a melting pot of cultures, ideas, and aspirations. Here, you'll find young minds debating serious issues in one corner while others laugh over *chai* and *samosas* in another. The market's atmosphere is an irresistible blend of the carefree exuberance of youth and the subtle undertones of ambition, making it a magnet for anyone seeking to experience the vibrant pulse of Delhi's student life.

Manohar navigated through the crowd, the vibrancy of the place momentarily distracting him from his thoughts. But as he reached Amit's door, the knot in his stomach returned. He rang the doorbell, and Amit opened it almost immediately, his face lighting up with a grin.

"Manohar! It's been a while. What brings you here? Or should I guess—you're here to see me and hoping for a glimpse of Prita?" Amit teased, his laugh echoing through the room.

Manohar chuckled, stepping inside. "A bit of both, maybe," he replied, trying to keep his tone light, though his thoughts were anything but light.

After a few minutes of casual conversation, Manohar steered the talk to what had been weighing on his mind. "Amit, I've been thinking about what you said yesterday... about Prita and her caste," he began hesitantly, his voice trailing off.

Amit leaned back in his chair, raising an eyebrow. "Still stuck on that, are you, pandit ji?" he said, using the nickname that poked fun at Manohar's traditional mindset. "Come on, if people like us don't challenge these barriers, who will?"

Manohar shifted uneasily. "It's not that simple, Amit. We've grown up being told to respect our parents' wishes. Isn't going against them... wrong?"

Amit's expression softened, but his voice carried a steely resolve. "Manohar, respecting your parents doesn't mean living their life. It's about living your own while honouring them. I love my family, but if I let outdated beliefs dictate my happiness, what's the point of my education? What's the point of thinking for myself?"

Manohar frowned, struggling to reconcile Amit's words with the traditions he had always known. "But traditions aren't meaningless, Amit. They're part of who we are."

"Sure," Amit replied, leaning forward, his tone sharp yet patient. "But aren't they also a way to keep us stuck? Look at my family—no one's ever married outside our caste. If I don't take a stand now, this cycle will keep spinning. Maybe I'll be the first domino to fall, but I'm okay with that if it means paving the way for something better."

Manohar stared at his friend, the sheer conviction in Amit's voice leaving him momentarily speechless. "And what about your parents? What if they disown you?" he finally asked, voicing the fear that had been gnawing at him.

Amit sighed, the weight of the question evident. "I've thought about that too, Manohar. I don't know how they'll react, but I'm prepared. If I back down now, I'll be letting fear win. Love isn't about caste or community—it's about understanding, respect, and building something real."

Manohar's mind was a whirlwind as he listened. Amit, from a wealthier, more progressive family, was prepared to risk everything. Meanwhile, Manohar, with fewer resources and a father whose expectations were less rigid, felt paralysed by the thought of defying tradition. The irony stung.

As he walked back through Kamla Nagar's crowded streets, Amit's words echoed in his ears: "If we don't take a stand, nothing will ever change." The chaos of the market seemed to mirror the turmoil inside him. Could he ever muster the courage to break free from the beliefs that had defined him? Could he make decisions as bold as Amit's?

Manohar didn't have the answers yet, but one thing was clear: Amit's resolve had ignited a spark in him–a spark that refused to be ignored.

The seeds of change had been planted, but whether they would grow in Manohar's heart remained to be seen.

Chapter 23

FAMILY STUNNED

Amit had always admired his father, Mr. Srivastava. He was a self-made man, a pillar in the community and a role model to his son. Everything Amit had been taught about respect, duty and tradition came from the foundation his father had built. That evening, as the sun sank behind the city skyline, Amit knew the conversation he was about to have would challenge everything. He wasn't just revealing his choice of a life partner; he was questioning the very norms that had defined his family's existence.

The family sat together in the living room, the soft bustle of evening fading into an uneasy silence. Mr. Srivastava, seated in his favourite armchair, was absorbed in the newspaper, while his mother busied herself in the kitchen, preparing the evening tea. Amit felt his heart race as he stood by his father, gathering the courage to break the news.

"Papa, I need to talk to you about something important," he said, his voice steady but his hands betraying his nervousness.

Mr. Srivastava lowered his newspaper, his eyes narrowing as he focused on his son. "What is it, Amit?" His voice was calm, but there was an underlying tension that hinted at the gravity of the conversation.

Amit paused, searching for the right words. "I've been thinking a lot about my future… and there's someone I want to marry."

His father's posture stiffened, his eyes locking on Amit's. "Marriage, Amit? You're still young. Focus on your career. You don't need to rush into anything."

Amit took a deep breath, knowing this moment was inevitable. "I've made up my mind, Papa. I want to marry Prita."

The room fell silent. Mr. Srivastava's face hardened, his expression unreadable as he absorbed the name. He had heard of Prita but never in the context of a marriage proposal. His mother, hearing the mention of the name, walked into the room, her hands holding a tray of tea, but her face was pale, sensing the weight of the conversation.

"Who is this Prita?" Mr. Srivastava asked, his voice sharp. "Is she from your institute?"

"Yes, Papa. She's doing the same course as me. We've been friends for a long time, and… I've come to love her," Amit replied, his tone unwavering.

"And what do you know about her family?" Mr. Srivastava's voice grew tense, his question cutting through the air. "You're telling me you want to marry someone whose background we know nothing about?"

Amit's resolve remained firm. "Papa, Prita's caste doesn't matter to me. What matters is who she is–her intelligence, her ambition, and her character."

The words hung in the air, thick with tension. Mr. Srivastava's face flushed with frustration. "You've lost your mind, Amit. Do you think values and ambition will erase the shame you'll bring upon this family? We've worked hard and built a reputation, and you're willing to throw it all away for this girl?"

Amit's voice didn't waver. "I'm not throwing anything away. I'm choosing my future, and Prita is part of it. She's more than just a name. She's the woman I love."

His mother, who had been silent up until now, spoke with a tremor in her voice, her eyes searching for some sign of her son's reasoning. "Amit, please... think about it. Marriage isn't just about love. It's about family and tradition. How will she fit into our lives? What will people say?"

Amit felt a pang of guilt, but he couldn't back down. "I've thought about all of it, *Maa*. It won't be easy, but I can't live my life based on what others think. I have to make my own choices."

Mr. Srivastava stood up suddenly, his voice rising with anger. "Choices? Do you think your mother and I didn't make sacrifices for you? We built this life for you and now you're willing to tear it down for some girl you barely know? What have we taught you all these years?"

Amit met his father's eyes, his resolve stronger than ever. "I respect everything you've done, Papa. But things are changing. The world is changing, and so are the traditions that define us. I can't live in a world where someone's caste decides their worth. Prita has worked hard to get where she is. That's what matters."

Mr. Srivastava's face twisted in disbelief. "You've gone mad, Amit. If you marry her, you'll be cut off. You'll have nothing left."

His mother's voice broke, and her tears welled up as she reached for her son's hand. "Please, Amit... don't do this to us. Think of your family, think of the future."

Amit's heart ached to see his mother in distress, but he knew what he had to do. He stood tall and said, "I love Prita, and I'm going to marry her."

The room fell into an eerie silence. The air was thick with the weight of his words. His mother's hands trembled as she reached out, her voice almost a whisper. "Amit... what does she even look like?"

Amit froze. He knew this moment would come, the moment when his mother would question Prita's appearance. He had avoided showing them Prita's photograph, fearing their reaction. Prita wasn't what his parents had envisioned for him—she wasn't conventionally beautiful, and her family wasn't wealthy. But none of that mattered to Amit.

He reached into his pocket, his fingers shaking, and pulled out a photograph. With a deep breath, he handed it to his mother. She took it with trembling hands, her eyes scanning the image. A moment passed before she looked up, her face drained of colour.

"She's not good-looking," his mother said softly, her words hanging heavily in the room. "How could you choose her? She's not from the right family. This isn't what we expected for you."

His father's voice followed, equally disapproving. "Amit, she doesn't have the background, the looks or the upbringing we've always valued. What are you thinking?"

Amit stood tall, his heart racing but his voice steady. "Mum, Dad, Prita may not meet your expectations, but she's the woman I love. She's strong and independent, and she's worked hard for everything she has. That's what matters to me."

His mother shook her head, unable to comprehend. "But, Amit, looks matter. Society will judge us."

"Let them," Amit said, his tone firm yet respectful. "I don't care about society's judgement. I care about Prita and the life we want to build together. I chose her for who she is, not for how she looks."

The silence in the room was deafening. Amit's parents sat stunned, their expressions a mix of disbelief and hurt. They had hoped their son would see reason, but Amit was unwavering. He knew this decision would change everything, but he also knew he had to follow his heart.

As he left the room, his parents were left to grapple with the reality that their son had chosen a path they could not understand.

When Manohar later heard about this confrontation, he was shocked. He had never imagined that Amit, coming from such a well-established family, would defy his parents so completely. Amit's determination to follow his heart, despite the fallout, left Manohar questioning his own courage.

Amit had done something Manohar wasn't sure he could. He had chosen love over tradition, and in doing so, had forced Manohar to confront his own beliefs about family, expectations, and the courage it takes to follow your heart.

For now, Manohar could only watch in awe, wondering if he could ever be as brave as his friend.

Chapter 24

HINDUSTAN TIMES

Manohar's year-long journalism course at Bhartiya Vidya Bhavan had drawn to a close, marking the end of one chapter and the beginning of the next. He had learned more than he had ever expected—ranging from the technicalities of reporting to the finer details of storytelling. More importantly, he had built a network of friends and mentors who had already begun to pave the way for him. With his degree now secured, Manohar was ready to step into the professional world.

It was clear to him that the next step was critical. He had already contributed articles to a few smaller magazines, seeing his by-line appear on the pages of local publications. That gave him some confidence, but he knew the real challenge was landing a position at a reputed media house—a place where true journalists thrived. *Hindustan Times*, with its long-standing legacy and prominence, was at the top of his list.

Situated on Kasturba Gandhi Marg, just a stone's throw away from his institute, *Hindustan Times* office had always seemed like a world apart—one that could only be accessed by those who had truly earned their place. It wasn't just a newspaper; it was a brand, an institution in its own right. Manohar had no doubts that securing an internship there was his gateway to something far bigger. But that was easier said than done.

❋　❋　❋

One evening, feeling both a sense of urgency and a spark of determination, Manohar decided to take action. Armed with little more than a phone number for the Managing Editor's office—one he had found after extensive digging—he set out for an STD booth near his flat. The air inside the booth smelled of stale sweat and cigarette smoke, the walls stained with years of neglect. The booth operator sat slumped in his chair, flipping through a tattered magazine, indifferent to the world around him.

Manohar dialled the number, his fingers trembling slightly. As the phone rang, his thoughts swirled with a mix of excitement and anxiety. He had no idea what to expect, but he knew he had to try.

"Good evening, madam," he greeted as the phone clicked on the other end.

A sharp, clipped voice responded almost immediately. "Evening. Who's this?"

"My name is Manohar," he began, "and I'm pursuing a degree in journalism. I was hoping to speak with Mr. Mitra about an internship opportunity."

There was a long pause before the voice came back, sounding tired. "Have you met him before?"

"No, madam," Manohar replied, trying to keep his voice steady.

"Well, Mr. Mitra is a very busy man," she snapped. "He doesn't have time for internship talks. Try someone else."

Manohar's heart sank, but he didn't give up. "I understand, but could you kindly give me the name and contact of someone else who handles internships?"

Another pause. A long one. Finally, she replied harshly, "I can't give you that information," before the call ended abruptly.

Manohar stood frozen for a moment, staring at the receiver in his hand. The emptiness of the dial tone echoed in his ear, and he fought the frustration building in his chest. He had expected this, but the sharpness of her response still stung.

After a few deep breaths, he dialled the number again. This time, there was no answer at all. Manohar remained standing in the booth for several minutes, his resolve beginning to waver, but still determined. Eventually, he hung up, feeling both defeated and enraged. But something inside him told him that giving up now would be the biggest mistake of all.

The next week, as soon as he had the chance, Manohar called again. And the week after that. Every call was met with the same cold reception—the same dismissive tone. But Manohar wasn't about to let go of this opportunity. His friends began to grow concerned, wondering why he was so fixated on the *Hindustan Times* when so many other options were available.

"Manohar, there are plenty of other newspapers you could try," his flatmate Rajan said one evening as they sat down for dinner. "Why keep calling the same place when they've already made it clear they're not interested? You're wasting your time."

Manohar was unfazed. "Because it's *Hindustan Times*, Rajan. It's not just any newspaper. It's the opportunity of a lifetime."

Rajan raised an eyebrow. "But they've rejected you every time. How long are you going to keep doing this?"

"As long as it takes," Manohar replied, his voice unwavering. "I'm not giving up."

And so, the weeks passed. Each call was a small victory, a testament to Manohar's relentless determination. His resolve never wavered, even when it seemed like the walls were closing in. He knew that persistence was the only thing that would eventually open the door. And so, he kept calling, his eyes firmly set on the prize ahead.

✻ ✻ ✻

It was just another press event, a sea of people rushing from one conversation to another, journalists scribbling notes, and public figures exchanging pleasantries. The clinking of glasses and the murmur of small talk filled the air, but Manohar was in his own little world. He had finished his freelance assignment for the day, his notepad filled with scribbles, and now he could take a breath. As he moved towards an empty chair beside a smart woman, he noticed she was writing notes as well.

They exchanged a quick greeting, and before long, their conversation shifted to the one thing that was on Manohar's mind—the elusive internship at the *Hindustan Times*.

"I've been trying to get through to the Managing Editor for a month now," he confessed, his voice tinged with frustration. "But his PA keeps blocking me. She won't even let me speak to him."

The woman's eyebrows shot up in surprise. "A month? And you're still chasing him?"

"Yes," Manohar sighed. "She just won't let me through."

The woman didn't respond immediately. Instead, she pulled out her phone with a calmness that was both reassuring and mystifying. She dialled the number without hesitation, pressing the phone to her ear. Manohar watched, half in awe, half in disbelief, as she spoke with an air of authority that made the whole room seem to quiet down.

"Hi, Mr. Mitra?" she said into the phone, her tone smooth and confident. "I'm sending someone over tomorrow at 5 p.m. for an internship. His name is Manohar. Please help him out."

She hung up, her gaze turning back to Manohar, who stood frozen, trying to process the fact that this stranger had just made the call he had been desperately trying to make for weeks.

"Tomorrow. 5 p.m. sharp in his office," she said, matter-of-factly. "If you have any trouble, just call me."

Manohar could hardly believe it. "I... I don't know how to thank you. This... this is amazing!" he stammered.

She waved it off with a smile, "No need. Just show up on time and make the most of it."

❋ ❋ ❋

The next afternoon, Manohar stood outside the towering *Hindustan Times* building on Kasturba Gandhi Marg, a full half hour early. The glass windows shimmered in the fading light of the evening, and the sheer size of the building was both intimidating and exciting. Inside, the lobby buzzed with the frantic energy of journalists rushing through their day—papers in hand, phones ringing, conversations in hushed tones. The smell of freshly printed ink lingered in the air, blending with the distant aroma of coffee.

Manohar couldn't help but feel out of place as he took in the surroundings. His simple clothes, his unpolished shoes—everything about him felt so... ordinary in comparison to the polished, fast-paced world of high-level journalism around him. He waited nervously, his heart thumping in his chest, until the elevator doors finally opened on the 7th floor.

There, at the reception desk, sat the PA–an effortlessly stylish woman with perfectly manicured nails tapping away on the desk, lost in conversation. Manohar took a deep breath and waited as patiently as he could. Ten minutes passed. Ten long minutes. Finally, she looked up, her gaze scanning him briefly before she asked, "Yes? Who are you here to meet?"

"I have an appointment with Mr. Mitra," Manohar said, trying to keep his voice steady. "Ms. Nisha told me to come."

The PA's eyes flicked up at the mention of Nisha's name. There was a moment of hesitation before she nodded. "Take a seat. I'll call Mr. Mitra."

Manohar sank into the plush sofa in the waiting area, his palms sweaty. He had no idea what was about to happen, but for the first time in weeks, he wasn't as anxious. He felt... ready.

Minutes later, the PA gestured for him to go inside. The moment had come.

❋   ❋   ❋

Manohar stepped into the office, and the immediate wave of cigarette smoke hit him like a wall. The room was dimly lit, cluttered with magazines, papers, and overflowing ashtrays. The scent of old tobacco mingled with the metallic tang of printers and fax machines in the corner. Mr. Mitra sat behind a massive desk, typing furiously on his keyboard, his salt-and-pepper hair reflecting the dull light of the room.

"Yes, come in," he said, without even looking up, his voice booming through the haze of smoke.

Manohar stepped forward, a little nervous but determined. He handed Mr. Mitra his CV and a file of his published work. Mr. Mitra barely glanced at them, flipping through the pages with practised ease before finally looking up.

"So, you want an internship?" he asked, his voice low and gravelly.

"Yes, Sir," Manohar said, trying to sound confident.

Mr. Mitra took a slow drag from his cigarette and blew out a cloud of smoke. "How about Patna?" he asked suddenly.

"Patna?" Manohar blinked in surprise but quickly nodded. "Yes, Sir. I can go there."

Mr. Mitra leaned back in his chair and smiled, a rare flicker of kindness crossing his face. "I'll let Mr. Talpatra in Patna know you're coming. You'll start there next week."

He handed the CV to his PA with instructions to fax it over. Then, as if it had all been a routine transaction, he looked back at Manohar. "Good luck, man. And say hi to Nisha for me."

The meeting had barely lasted five minutes, but it felt like a lifetime to Manohar. He had done it. He had finally secured the internship.

✳ ✳ ✳

As Manohar left the building, the cool evening air hit his face like a rush of fresh air. A wave of relief washed over him, followed by the sweet sensation of accomplishment. His persistence had paid off. He wasn't just a student anymore; he was about to step into the real world of journalism.

As he walked towards the bus stop, the city around him seemed to buzz with new energy. For the first time in weeks, Manohar felt a sense of peace. He had taken the first step towards his dream, and this was just the beginning.

Chapter 25

JOURNEY TO PATNA

Manohar's heart raced as he left Mr. Mitra's office. His dream had been set in motion: an internship at the *Hindustan Times'* Patna office. It was a rare opportunity that could propel his career in journalism. The excitement, however, was tempered by a familiar challenge—getting a train ticket to Bihar. Travel to Patna in the '90s wasn't as simple as booking a seat online; it was an ordeal that required patience, persistence, and often, extra money.

Securing a seat on a Bihar-bound train during the busy season was almost an impossibility, especially with reservations always full weeks in advance. The only way to get a ticket was through the infamous network of ticket agents, notorious for charging hefty premiums. With time slipping away and urgency mounting, Manohar had no choice but to pay nearly double the regular fare.

As he packed his bag the night before his departure, he couldn't help but smile bitterly at the irony. He was about to begin an internship with one of the most prominent media houses in the country, and yet, here he was—paying extra for a train ticket. It seemed that even the path to success had its tolls.

The journey itself was a far cry from the comfortable ride he had imagined. The compartments were crowded, and the train hummed with the sounds of vendors hawking everything from biscuits to newspapers. The air was thick with the mingling scent of sweat, tea, and dust. Yet, amidst it all, Manohar's thoughts were focused on the future. He knew that once he reached Patna, everything could change. This internship was his chance to make a name for himself in the world of journalism, and no matter how uncomfortable the journey, it would be worth it.

Manohar stepped off the train early the next morning at Patna Junction, greeted by the chaotic energy of the station. It was the kind of bustling scene that felt familiar to anyone who had travelled in India—porters carrying enormous loads on their heads, families gathered at platforms waiting for their loved ones, and vendors calling out their wares. Amidst this frenzy stood the Lord Hanuman Temple, its serene presence offering a brief respite from the chaos of the station. The scent of marigold flowers, Tirupati's famous *ladoos*, mixed with the incense as early morning devotees knelt to pray.

For a moment, Manohar stood still, his eyes on the temple. He folded his hands, seeking a moment of quiet reflection. Perhaps, he thought, a prayer for good fortune in the days ahead wouldn't hurt.

At exactly 10 a.m., Manohar stood before the unassuming office of *Hindustan Times* in Patna. Unlike the towering, sleek structure in Delhi, this building was modest, its cream-coloured walls showing the wear of years. The office was small, and the hustle and bustle of journalists was replaced with a more subdued rhythm. The street outside was quieter, and bicycles, rather than cars, lined the perimeter.

He walked in, introduced himself to the security guard, and was directed to Mr. Talpatra's office. After a tense hour of waiting, he was finally summoned.

"Good morning, Sir," Manohar greeted as he entered the office.

"Good morning," Mr. Talpatra responded curtly without looking up from his papers. The room was lined with stacks of magazines and files, and a thin haze of cigarette smoke lingered in the air. "Manohar, is it?"

Manohar nodded.

"You're here for an internship. Do you have any published work?" Mr. Talpatra asked, not even lifting his eyes from the papers.

Manohar pushed a file of articles towards him. Talpatra flipped through the pages with mechanical precision, offering a murmured "good" every now and then. But then his hand paused on one particular article. He read it more carefully, his expression shifting.

"Where was this article published?" Talpatra asked sharply, his gaze now fixed on Manohar.

"*The Pioneer*, Sir," Manohar replied, his chest swelling with pride.

Talpatra set the article down, leaning back in his chair. "Are you a Brahmin?"

"Yes, Sir. Maithili Brahmin," Manohar replied, unsure where the conversation was headed.

A faint, knowing smirk appeared on Talpatra's face. "Ah, I see. That explains the attitude reflected in this article."

Manohar felt a knot tighten in his stomach. "What's wrong with the article, Sir?" he asked, his voice now quieter, more cautious.

Talpatra leaned forward, his voice rising slightly. "Nothing's wrong, per se. But your approach is clearly biased. You've written from a position of privilege, Mr. Manohar. You're defending a caste system that has oppressed millions. Your words reek of Brahmin superiority."

Manohar was taken aback. "Sir, I didn't mean to come across as biased. I was simply trying to highlight the historical structure..."

"History is written by those in power," Talpatra interrupted, his voice sharp. "The system you're defending is the very system that continues to marginalise people like me. You talk about the caste system as if it's a relic of the past, but for people like us, it's a daily reality. The Mandal Commission was a turning point, and yet you write about it as though the Brahmins are the victims."

Manohar sat frozen, his mind racing. This wasn't a conversation about journalism anymore. It was personal. Talpatra continued, delving into the nuances of caste discrimination, the reservation system, and the role of privilege. Manohar was left grappling with the harsh truths he'd never fully considered.

✻ ✻ ✻

Eventually, Talpatra stood up, signalling the end of the meeting. "I'll discuss this with Mr. Mitra and get back to you," he said, offering no more than a brief nod.

Manohar thanked him, but the weight of the conversation lingered in his mind as he left the office. The internship—his dream—seemed more uncertain than ever.

Walking back to his hotel, doubt gnawed at him. Had his article truly been a defence of the caste system? Was he wrong to have written from his perspective, shaped by his upbringing? The questions swirled in his head, and for the first time, he found himself questioning not just his article, but his very identity.

✻ ✻ ✻

Manohar returned to Delhi, his heart heavy with uncertainty. Days turned into weeks, then into a month. But no letter came. No phone call. His friends tried to console him, telling him it was just a delay, but deep down, he knew the truth.

The article–the one he thought was a simple reflection of his thoughts–had cost him the internship. And in the process, it had opened a door he wasn't yet ready to walk through. The harshness of caste, the divisions he had long ignored, now seemed inescapable.

Manohar sat in silence, waiting for something—anything—that would bring him closure. But for the first time, he knew he had to confront more than just his career. He had to confront his own beliefs.

Chapter 26

A JOURNEY CONTINUED

Manohar was no stranger to setbacks, but the sting of missing out on the coveted internship at *Hindustan Times* was sharper than he had anticipated. The rejection was a bitter pill to swallow, especially after the effort he had put into his application and the long waits. But as much as it distressed him, it didn't break his spirit. He wasn't the type to dwell on failures for too long. The world was vast, and opportunities were everywhere—he just had to find them.

It was during one of his many sleepless nights, mulling over what to do next, that he came across a glimmer of hope. An advertisement in *The Times of India* caught his eye: a national magazine based in Noida was looking for editorial staff. The prospect of a full-time position at this magazine was no mere chance—it was an opportunity he had been waiting for, especially since he had been contributing freelance work for months. His editor, always complimentary about his sharp insights, had once hinted that should a position open up, Manohar would be at the top of the list.

It felt like the right time to take that leap.

The first thing Manohar did when he saw the advertisement was to call his editor. The conversation was brief but encouraging. "You've done well for us so far," his editor said, "but remember, competition will be fierce. Thousands will apply, and it's out of my hands. If you're serious, give it your all."

Manohar left the conversation feeling a mix of excitement and anxiety. He didn't know if this would be the moment that changed everything, but he was going to give it his best shot. His mind buzzed with possibilities as he made his way to the magazine's Noida office the next day. The building was far less imposing than the grand offices he had once imagined working in. It was modest, located in the industrial heart of Noida, with journalists huddled around computers, scribbling on notepads, or rushing between phones and desks. It was a world far removed from the glamorous image of journalism he had once dreamed of, but it was alive with energy—a feeling he instantly connected with.

When he stepped into his editor's cabin, it felt strangely familiar yet profoundly different. The editor greeted him warmly, asking about his intentions. Manohar wasted no time and asked about the process, eager to prepare for the upcoming exam and interview.

"The competition is stiff," the editor warned again, leaning back in his chair, "but I believe in your abilities. Just focus on the exam, and do your best."

With a mixture of hope and nerves, Manohar left the office that day, knowing that this would be a defining moment in his journey.

Back in his small rented room in Delhi, the preparation began in earnest. He was no stranger to hard work, but this felt different. It wasn't just another writing assignment. This was his future. He immersed himself in every available resource—newspapers, books, essays—anything that would give him an edge. Nights were spent in the dim glow of a flickering tube light, with the air in his room growing thick with the smell of coffee and anxiety. His thoughts often turned inward, revisiting his freelance experiences, questioning how well he had done, and wondering if it was enough to get him through the written exam.

The exam day arrived with a certain heaviness in the air. The exam hall was packed with candidates, all of them hoping for the same thing: a chance to prove themselves. The pressure was palpable, but Manohar felt an unusual calmness as he navigated through the three sections: current affairs, journalistic ethics, and a writing task. The questions were tough, and time seemed to slip away faster than he anticipated, but his freelance experience gave him the confidence he needed. When the bell rang to signify the end of the exam, Manohar felt a quiet sense of satisfaction—he had done everything he could.

Weeks passed before the letter finally arrived–an invitation to an interview. Manohar's pulse quickened when he read it. The competition, he knew, would be fierce, but this was his chance. He had to make it count.

The night before the interview, he hardly slept. He studied until his eyes burned, flipping through newspapers and magazines, trying to get a grip on every bit of current news. As the morning sun peeked through his window, he prepared himself meticulously. The borrowed cream-coloured shirt he wore felt a little snug, and the tie he fumbled with in the mirror seemed more of a nuisance than an accessory. But he straightened his shoulders, adjusted the knot one last time, and walked out of his room with a mixture of dread and anticipation.

The magazine's office was a place he knew well, yet walking through its doors this time felt different. He wasn't just a contributor now. He was a candidate, and the weight of that responsibility pressed down on him. The waiting area was quiet, save for the soft clicking of keyboards and the rustling of papers. His hand instinctively went to adjust his tie again, exuding his anxiety despite the calm exterior he tried to project. Every tick of the clock seemed to drag on, heightening his anticipation.

When his name was finally called, he entered the interview room to find three senior editors and the company director sitting in front of him. He felt the familiar warmth of his editor's gaze as he sat down, but the weight of the other eyes on him made his heart beat a little faster.

During the interview, Manohar's hand betrayed him, repeatedly straying to the knot of his tie as though it held the key to his composure. Each time his fingers brushed against the fabric, he was reminded of the restless night he had spent preparing, poring over newspapers and practising responses. What started as a reassuring gesture soon became a nervous tic, one he couldn't seem to control. The more he tried to suppress it, the more his self-consciousness grew. It was as if his nerves had decided to stage a rebellion, exposing his anxiety in a room where he desperately wanted to appear confident.

The questions came steadily, probing his knowledge, his aspirations, and his vision for the future of journalism. Manohar answered with careful deliberation, drawing from his freelance experiences and countless late nights spent honing his craft. Yet, the tie seemed to tighten with each passing moment, its snug knot a silent witness to his inner turmoil.

Halfway through, the editor leaned back in his chair with a knowing smile. "Manohar," he said, his voice warm yet steady, "I must tell you something."

Manohar's hand froze mid-air, caught in its habitual reach for the tie.

"Out of 5,000 candidates, you've ranked at the very top."

Manohar blinked, the words taking a moment to sink in. "The top?" he repeated, incredulous.

"Yes," the editor said, his smile widening. "Your written exam was outstanding. You outperformed every single one of them."

The room seemed to shift as a wave of relief washed over him, his earlier nerves dissolving into an almost surreal pride. All those sleepless nights, the tireless preparation—it had paid off in a way he hadn't dared to imagine.

"But," the editor added, his tone softening, "The process is not complete. You've done incredibly well so far, but there are a few more steps to go."

Manohar nodded, his earlier jitters replaced by a renewed sense of purpose. As he left the office that day, the oppressive weight of uncertainty had lifted, replaced by the realisation that his dream was now within reach.

✳ ✳ ✳

A month later, under the relentless blaze of the summer sun, the sound of the doorbell pierced the stillness of the afternoon.

Ding-dong!

"Manohar Kumar!" a voice called out from below, booming with urgency.

Manohar, who had been sifting through his notes in his modest room, shot to his feet. His heart raced as he bounded down the narrow, creaky staircase. At the gate stood a middle-aged postman, his weathered face partially hidden under the shadow of his cap. He held a brown envelope, its corners slightly creased.

"Registered post," the man said, handing the envelope over. "Sign here."

Manohar grabbed the envelope, his hands trembling as he scribbled his signature. His excitement was barely contained. The postman tipped his cap and walked away, leaving Manohar standing at the gate with his prize in hand.

He bolted back upstairs, clutching the envelope as though it were a sacred relic. Once inside, he paused, staring at it as if the contents might vanish if he acted too hastily. Finally, with deliberate care, he tore it open. His eyes skimmed the letter, and then—

"I've got it!" he shouted, his voice breaking the silence of the room.

It was the appointment letter. The magazine had offered him the editorial position he had dreamed of. For a moment, he simply sat there, the letter pressed against his chest, his eyes brimming with tears. Years of rejection, relentless effort, and unwavering belief had culminated in this one moment.

The date, June 8th, etched itself into his memory. It was a day of significance—a day that seemed destined to mark turning points in his life.

Manohar's journey from a determined freelance writer to the top-ranked candidate for an editorial role wasn't just a career milestone; it was a testament to his resilience. The path ahead would undoubtedly be filled with challenges, but for the first time, he felt that his childhood dream of becoming a journalist wasn't just an aspiration—it was a reality he was now living. With the letter in hand and a world of possibilities unfolding before him, Manohar knew one thing: this was only the beginning of something extraordinary.

Chapter 27

MOVING TO NOIDA

As Manohar handed the box of sweets to Simran, pride swelled in his chest. Yet, beneath that pride was a subtle tug of hesitation, an unshakeable feeling he couldn't quite name. Simran accepted the box, her fingers brushing the bright, celebratory wrapper and lingering for a moment longer than necessary. Her hands trembled ever so slightly, betraying emotions she tried hard to mask.

"Sir, I knew this day would come," she said softly, her voice steady but her smile faltering. She carefully opened the box, her movements deliberate, as though stalling for time. Picking out a piece of the sugary treat, she offered it to Manohar. "You were always meant for something greater."

Manohar took the sweet with a grateful nod, but the first bite didn't bring the joy he had expected. The sugar seemed cloying, its sweetness hollow against the weight pressing on his chest. He watched Simran closely, noticing the shadows in her usually bright eyes, the faint strain at the corners of her mouth.

"Thank you, Simran," he said quietly, his voice tinged with something unspoken. "But there's something else I need to tell you."

Simran froze, her hand resting on the edge of the box, as though bracing herself for the words she sensed were coming. "What is it, Sir?"

Manohar took a deep breath, his fingers curling into fists at his sides. "With this new job... I'll have to move to Noida. It's too far to commute from here."

Simran's world seemed to stop. The words hung in the air, heavy and unyielding. She blinked, as though trying to make sense of them. "Noida?" she repeated, her voice soft, tinged with disbelief. "You're leaving?"

Her tone was childlike, almost pleading, and it struck a chord deep within Manohar. He had rehearsed this conversation a dozen times, but standing here now, it felt all wrong. It felt like abandonment. "Yes, Simran," he said, his voice steady but low. "I have to. The magazine's office is there, and the commute would be impossible. I'll be moving next month."

She bit her lip, her eyes fixed on the sweets she was no longer seeing. "But it won't be the same without you here, Sir," she whispered, her voice breaking despite her efforts to stay composed. She didn't want to sound selfish or weak, but the thought of him being gone, of not seeing him every day, left an ache she couldn't ignore.

Manohar's gaze softened, and he felt a pang of guilt. He had worked so hard for this job, yet the cost of it now seemed unbearably high. "I'll miss it too," he admitted, his voice almost a whisper. "I'll miss you, Simran. But this job—it's important for my future."

Simran nodded slowly, her forced smile not reaching her eyes. "Of course, Sir. You deserve this. You've worked so hard…" Her voice trailed off, and she looked away, blinking rapidly as though willing herself not to cry.

"Just what?" Manohar asked gently, sensing there was more she wanted to say.

She hesitated, her fingers busying themselves with the sweets again, a futile attempt to distract herself. Finally, she spoke, her voice barely audible. "It's just… you've been more than a mentor to me, Sir. You've been someone I could rely on, someone who… understands me in a way no one else does. I don't know how to explain it, but your leaving feels like losing a part of myself."

Her voice cracked, and she quickly bit down on her lip, trying to hold back tears.

Manohar's heart clenched at her words. He hadn't realised how much he meant to her, how deeply she valued their bond. For a moment, he struggled to find the right words. "Simran… you're not losing me," he said finally. "I'm just moving to Noida, not disappearing. We'll still see each other. I'll visit, and we can stay in touch."

Simran shook her head slowly, a single tear escaping down her cheek. "But it won't be the same, Sir," she whispered, turning her face away. "You know it won't."

The silence that followed was thick with unspoken emotions, the weight of change settling over them both. Manohar knew she was right. It wouldn't be the same. No words of reassurance could change that. Moving to

Noida felt like a step forward in his career, but it also felt like leaving behind something he couldn't quite define—something fragile yet profound.

"I'm happy for you, Sir. Truly," Simran said after a moment, her voice trembling but sincere. "You deserve this more than anyone I know."

Manohar stepped closer, his hand resting lightly on her shoulder. "You don't have to say goodbye, Simran. Not yet. I'm still here for a little while. And even after I move... I'll always be there for you."

She looked up at him, her tear-filled eyes searching his face for reassurance. "Promise me you won't forget about me once you're gone."

Manohar smiled softly, though his heart felt heavy. "I could never forget you, Simran. You've been an important part of my life too. More than you realise."

For a long moment, they stood in silence, the unspoken emotions between them filling the room. It was a moment of bittersweet clarity—a celebration of Manohar's success tinged with the sorrow of impending separation. As the reality of the change settled over them, both understood that while some bonds are tested by distance, they remain unbroken, etched deeply in the heart.

I LOVE YOU FOREVER

The sun hadn't yet risen fully, but Manohar was already awake. His room was packed with suitcases, every corner holding memories and echoes of his journey. Noida awaited him, a new chapter in his life, yet the thought of leaving tugged at his heart. There was one final thing he had to do before embarking on this journey. He couldn't leave without saying goodbye to the Malhotra family. They weren't just a family that had helped him—they had become his family.

Standing outside their door, Manohar hesitated for a moment, his hand hovering over the bell. The faint scent of jasmine from the garden mixed with the stillness of the morning air. He finally pressed the bell. Moments later, the door opened to reveal Mrs. Malhotra, her familiar, warm face lighting up at the sight of him.

"Manohar *beta*," she greeted with a smile that was tinged with bittersweet pride. "Come in."

"Aunty," Manohar began, his voice steady but carrying an undertone of sadness, "I'm leaving tomorrow morning."

Mrs. Malhotra's smile faltered slightly. "Tomorrow? So soon?" she asked, her voice soft. She stepped aside to let him in. "Have you arranged everything? Your flat, the commute?"

"Yes, Aunty," he replied. "It's a small place, but it's close to the office. I'll manage."

Before Mrs. Malhotra could ask more, she called out, "Simran! Come quickly. Manohar is here."

Simran appeared moments later, her dupatta trailing behind her. Her face, usually bright with a hint of mischief, seemed subdued, her eyes shadowed with an emotion she couldn't quite mask. She looked at Manohar and tried to speak, but her voice wavered. "Sir, you're leaving tomorrow morning?"

"Yes, Simran," he answered gently. "It's time. I start the job day after tomorrow."

Simran nodded, her fingers nervously twisting the edge of her dupatta. She had known this moment was coming, yet the finality of it struck her deeply. "How far is your office from the flat?" she asked, trying to keep the conversation casual.

"Fifteen, maybe twenty minutes by bus," Manohar said, studying her face. "It's manageable."

The room fell silent, the weight of unspoken words hanging heavily in the air. Sensing the moment, Mrs. Malhotra excused herself. "I'll be in the kitchen," she said softly, leaving them alone.

Manohar turned to Simran, his voice filled with gratitude. "Simran, I want to thank you and your parents. I wouldn't have made it this far without your support."

"You don't need to thank us, Sir," she replied, her voice quiet but steady. "You've worked so hard. We only did what anyone would for family."

The word "family" hung in the air, a poignant reminder of their bond. Manohar stepped closer, his gaze sincere. "You and your parents have been more than just kind to me, Simran. You gave me a home, a place where I felt I belonged."

Simran's throat tightened. She fought back tears but couldn't stop her voice from trembling. "But now you're leaving, Sir. Everything will be different."

Manohar's own emotions threatened to overwhelm him, but he kept his composure. "Change doesn't mean an end, Simran. I'll come back to visit. We'll stay in touch."

"It feels like goodbye," she whispered, her words barely audible.

Manohar took a deep breath, his own heart heavy. "It's not goodbye forever, Simran. You're strong, and you have so much ahead of you."

Simran looked at him, her eyes brimming with tears. "I can't imagine you not being around, Sir."

Manohar smiled gently, his own eyes moist. "I'll always be there for you, Simran. Maybe not physically, but in spirit. You have my office number and you have my trust."

"Promise me," she said, her voice fragile.

"I promise," he replied, his words filled with sincerity.

For a moment, neither spoke. The silence was filled with all the emotions they couldn't put into words. Finally, as Manohar turned to leave, Simran's voice stopped him.

"Sir," she called out, her tone trembling.

He turned back, his expression soft yet questioning. "Yes, Simran?"

Her heart raced, her cheeks flushed. She summoned every ounce of courage, knowing this was her last chance to speak her truth. "I... I love you forever," she said, her voice breaking but resolute.

The world seemed to pause. Manohar stood frozen, caught off guard by the raw honesty in her confession. His mind raced, a whirlwind of emotions flooding him—admiration for her bravery, an overwhelming sense of gratitude, and a deep ache for the complexities that bound and separated them.

Tears streamed down Simran's face, but she quickly wiped them away, her gaze dropping to the floor. "I just wanted you to know," she whispered, her voice barely audible.

Manohar stepped closer, his own eyes glistening. He placed a hand gently on her shoulder. "Simran…" he began, his voice thick with unspoken emotion. "I'll always carry your words with me."

With that, he turned and walked out of the door. Simran stood motionless, watching him disappear down the street, a quiet resolve settling in her heart. She knew life would never be the same, but in her confession, she had found a piece of herself she hadn't known existed.

As Manohar walked away, the morning sun bathed the streets in a soft glow. It felt like an ending, but deep down, both knew it was also the beginning of something that words could never fully capture.

Chapter 29

EMOTIONAL STRUGGLE

Simran lay on her bed, the soft buzz of the ceiling fan above her doing little to dispel the heaviness in the room. Her heart thudded in her chest, and her mind was a whirlwind of emotions she couldn't tame. The words she had spoken to Manohar that day haunted her: "Sir, I love you forever."

The sheer weight of that confession felt unbearable now. She had imagined a hundred scenarios, but none of them prepared her for the reality of his silence. Was it shock? Indifference? Or something worse?

She stared at her phone, which was lying next to her. For minutes, she wrestled with herself before finally dialling the number of the one person who might understand her turmoil: her best friend, Riya.

"Hello?" Riya's chirpy voice greeted her, a stark contrast to Simran's sombre mood.

"Riya..." Simran's voice wavered. "I need to talk."

Immediately, Riya's tone softened. "What's wrong?"

"I told him," Simran blurted out, her chest tightening.

"Told him? Wait, him as in... Manohar?"

"Yes," she whispered, tears threatening to spill.

Riya inhaled sharply. "Okay. Wow! So… what happened? What did he say?"

Simran let out a shaky breath. "He didn't say anything. He just looked at me, like I'd said something… impossible. It was like he couldn't believe what he was hearing."

Riya paused before replying carefully, "That doesn't mean anything bad, Simran. Maybe he just needs time to process it. You know how he is—reserved, thoughtful."

Simran sat up, clutching the phone tightly. "What if I ruined everything? What if he never sees me the same way again? I can't stop thinking about it, Riya. What if I've made a fool of myself?"

The silence on the other end of the line felt heavy. Simran imagined Riya carefully choosing her words, trying to find a balance between honesty and comfort.

"Simran," Riya began gently, "you did what most people can't. You were honest about your feelings. That's brave. You put your heart out there, and that takes courage."

"But what if it's all for nothing?" Simran's voice cracked, her vulnerability spilling out like water from a broken dam. "I don't even know if he would ever feel the same way about me. What if I'm just a student to him? What if…" Her voice faltered. "What if he starts avoiding me?"

"Listen to me," Riya interjected firmly. "Manohar isn't the kind of person to disrespect your feelings. He's not going to avoid you, Simran. He respects you too much for that. Whatever happens, your relationship won't just disappear."

"But what if I've misread everything? What if all those moments I thought meant something... didn't?"

Simran's voice dropped to a whisper as she admitted, "I thought I'd feel relieved after telling him, but I don't. I feel... exposed. Vulnerable. Like I've given him this piece of me that I can never take back."

Riya sighed, her empathy palpable even through the phone. "Of course, you feel that way. You've been holding this in for so long. But Simran, love isn't about guarantees. It's about taking risks."

Simran closed her eyes, her tears finally escaping. "I just don't know if I'm strong enough to face his answer if it's not what I hope for."

"And you might not know for a while," Riya said softly. "But, Simran, don't let your fears take away from the courage you showed. Whatever happens, you'll be okay. I promise."

After the call ended, Simran sat in the quiet of her room, feeling both comforted and hollow. Her eyes wandered to the window, where the first stars had begun to dot the night sky. The stillness of the night was a sharp contrast to the chaos within her.

She clutched her pillow tightly, her thoughts spiralling back to Manohar. Was he thinking of her too? Did her words replay in his mind the way his stunned expression replayed in hers? Or had he already made peace with the fact that they could never be more than what they were?

Her heart ached with questions that only he could answer.

As the moonlight filtered into her room, she lay back on the bed, lost in her thoughts. She wanted to believe Riya's words that her bravery wouldn't be in vain. But as she drifted off to sleep, doubt clung to her like a shadow.

Somewhere, she hoped that Manohar, too, was lying awake, grappling with the same uncertainty.

Chapter 30

INTERNAL CONFLICT

The night was calm, yet Manohar's mind churned with a storm of emotions. He sat at his modest desk, the flickering light of a solitary lamp casting long shadows on the walls. Before him lay his open journal, its blank pages a stark contrast to the chaos within him. His pen hovered above the paper, but no words came. The thoughts swirling in his head were too fragmented, too conflicting, to be confined to ink.

"Sir, I love you forever."

Simran's voice echoed in his memory, the earnestness in her words piercing through his defences. Those words had a way of clinging to him, resurfacing in moments of quiet when he least expected them. It wasn't just the confession that unsettled him—it was the raw sincerity in her eyes and the way her trembling voice carried the weight of her feelings. Simran, his student, had become more than just a bright young mind to him. Her words had unearthed emotions he hadn't dared to acknowledge.

Manohar tried to focus, gripping the pen tighter as if sheer willpower could transform his tangled emotions into coherent thoughts. But his hand trembled, and the pen fell to the desk with a soft thud. He leaned back in his chair, letting out a sigh that felt too heavy for the stillness of the room. His journal had always been his confidant, a place where he could wrestle with his fears and uncertainties. Tonight, however, even this trusted refuge failed him.

On the surface, everything seemed to be falling into place. His career was finally taking shape, and the opportunity in Noida was a significant milestone. Yet, beneath the polished exterior, his heart was a battlefield. He cared deeply for Simran—there was no use denying it anymore. But towering between them was an invisible wall, built brick by brick over decades of tradition, familial duty, and societal expectations.

Tradition. Family. Society.

These words lingered in his mind like a judge's gavel, rendering silent verdicts that echoed through generations. They were not just concepts; they were chains, binding him to an identity he had never questioned—until now. Simran's love, her unguarded declaration, had cracked open something within him, forcing him to confront the uncomfortable question: Could love truly transcend these barriers?

Manohar ran a hand through his hair, his frustration mounting. He needed clarity, a perspective unclouded by his emotions. Picking up his phone, he hesitated for a moment before dialling a number he knew by heart. Mr. Rao, his older colleague and mentor, had always been a source of wisdom. If anyone could help him navigate this maze, it was him.

The phone rang only twice before Mr. Rao's deep, reassuring voice answered. "Manohar, my boy! What a pleasant surprise. How are you?"

"Good evening, Sir," Manohar began, his voice steadying as he spoke. "I hope I'm not disturbing you, but I... I need your advice."

"Of course, my boy. Tell me what's troubling you."

Manohar hesitated, his thoughts scrambling for a coherent starting point. Finally, he said, "Sir, how do you reconcile love and duty when they seem to stand on opposite sides? How do you choose?"

There was a pause, and then Mr. Rao chuckled, a warm, knowing sound. "Ah, the age-old conflict. Love and duty are two forces that rarely align as neatly as we'd like. But, Manohar, what's really weighing on you?"

Manohar felt a lump rise in his throat. This was the moment to lay bare his fears. "There's someone I care about deeply, Sir," he began, his voice faltering slightly. "She feels the same way about me. But... she's not from my caste. My family, our traditions—they expect me to marry within the boundaries set by them. I feel torn between what my heart wants and what I owe to my family."

Silence hung in the air before Mr. Rao spoke, his tone contemplative. "It's never an easy choice, is it? The heart whispers one thing, while the world we're part of shouts another. But tell me this: What kind of life do you see for yourself—a life shaped by the expectations of others or one where your heart finds peace?"

Manohar leaned forward, gripping the phone tighter as if the answer lay within Mr. Rao's words. "I don't know, Sir. I want to honour my family—they've done so much for me. But Simran… she's become such an important part of my life. I just don't know if I have the courage to go against everything I've been taught."

Mr. Rao's voice softened, his tone filled with understanding. "Manohar, courage isn't about defying everything you've known. It's about making a choice you can live with. Tradition can provide comfort, yes, but love— it's what gives life its true meaning. Sometimes, following your heart doesn't mean dishonouring your family. It means honouring the person you are and the life you want to lead."

Manohar sat in silence, letting the words sink in. Mr. Rao's insight didn't offer him a solution, but it gave him a lens through which he could view his dilemma. His feelings for Simran weren't just an inconvenient truth; they were a call to question the life he thought he was meant to live.

"Thank you, Sir," he said finally, his voice heavy with emotion. "I don't have the answers yet, but what you've said… it helps."

"Take your time, Manohar," Mr. Rao replied gently. "Decisions like these aren't made in a day. Just remember, whatever you choose, it should be a choice you can live with, one that lets you look back with pride, not regret."

Manohar rubbed his forehead, the pressure of indecision bearing down on him like a storm cloud. "But what if I can't have both? What if choosing one means losing the other?" His voice was steady, but the anguish behind it was unmistakable.

"That's the hard part, isn't it?" Mr. Rao's tone carried the weight of a man who had faced similar crossroads in his life. "Life often demands sacrifices. Sometimes it's duty; sometimes it's desire. But in the end, you have to ask yourself—what will bring you peace?"

Manohar thanked Mr. Rao and ended the call, the warmth in his mentor's words failing to dispel the cold fog in his mind. Instead of clarity, the conversation had unearthed a deeper sense of conflict, leaving him more torn than ever.

He leaned back in his chair, staring at the blank notebook before him. A part of him felt tethered to the traditions that had shaped his upbringing. He had always prided himself on being a dutiful son, following the unwritten rules that governed his family and community. But Simran had upended that certainty. Her confession wasn't just a declaration of love—it was a question aimed directly at the heart of who he was and what he truly wanted.

Manohar stood and moved to the window, pressing his palms against the cool glass. The city stretched out before him, a maze of glittering lights that seemed alive with stories, dreams, and struggles. Somewhere in that vast web of lives was Simran. He pictured her face, the trembling of her voice as she had said, "I love you forever." The memory was vivid—her tear-filled eyes, the quaver in her words, and the courage it had taken for her to expose her heart so completely.

The weight of it tugged at him. How could he not feel something for someone so genuine, so vulnerable? Yet with that tug came the suffocating weight of tradition. He imagined his parents' faces if they knew. Their disappointment. The stern rebuke that would follow. The unspoken but powerful verdict of their silence. Could he bear to become the son who broke the rules, who turned his back on their expectations for love?

His hands curled into fists as frustration bubbled inside him. He was a man of logic, someone who had always approached life's challenges with careful thought and measured steps. But this was different. There was no neat resolution here, no path that wouldn't demand a sacrifice. The question wasn't just about what others wanted from him—it was about what he could live with. Could he let go of Simran, knowing the depth of her love for him? Or would holding onto her come at the cost of losing his family's respect and the stability of the life he had always known?

He sighed, his breath fogging the glass. The longer he stood there, staring out at the city, the more he realised that this wasn't merely a battle between love and duty. It was a battle within himself—a struggle between the person he had been raised to be and the man he was slowly becoming. Tradition felt like a fortress, sturdy and familiar, but Simran's love was a force that made him question whether that fortress was also a cage.

Closing his eyes, Manohar leaned his forehead against the windowpane. The city buzzed on, indifferent to his turmoil. He thought of the many nights he had spent seeking solace in his journal, spilling out his thoughts in the hope of untangling them. Tonight, even his pen had failed him. The words wouldn't come because there was no easy resolution to this conflict.

He drew a deep breath, the cool air filling his lungs. The answers wouldn't come tonight. He knew that. Perhaps they wouldn't come tomorrow or even the day after. But he held onto a fragile hope that, in time, clarity would find him. For now, all he could do was sit with the heaviness of his thoughts, let the questions echo within him, and search for the strength to face whatever choice lay ahead.

The dawn was still hours away, but Manohar knew he was standing at the edge of a new beginning. Whether he would step forward or retreat remained uncertain, but one thing was clear—this decision would shape the rest of his life.

Chapter 31

NEW BEGINNINGS

Noida had a different pulse than Delhi. It wasn't the ceaseless chaos of the capital but a quieter hum, one that hinted at opportunity and ambition. For Manohar, the first few days in his new flat passed in a whirlwind of unpacking boxes, signing paperwork and scouting out the local markets. His one-bedroom apartment was modest, the walls bare and the furniture sparse, but it was his. For the first time, he had a space entirely his own. No more crowded lodges or shared rooms. Here, he was free to shape his life as he saw fit.

The mornings were a revelation. He would wake early, brew a steaming cup of tea, and sit by the window as the first light of day stretched over the city. The sight of the sun climbing above the horizon filled him with a tentative sense of hope. It felt like a fresh start, a chance to carve out his future. Yet, as the golden light spilt across the room, it carried with it a subtle ache—a reminder of his solitude. Independence, he quickly learned, came at a cost.

In the quiet of those early days, loneliness began to creep in. The bustling companionship of Delhi seemed a world away: the laughter of friends over shared meals, the familiar chaos of crowded streets, and most painfully, the comforting knowledge that Simran was just a short distance away. Here in Noida, even her memory felt distant, like a fading echo he couldn't quite chase.

Manohar couldn't shake the thought of her—her tear-filled eyes, her trembling voice as she confessed, "Sir, I love you forever." That moment replayed in his mind like a song stuck on a loop, each replay stirring something deep inside him. Had he made a mistake by not addressing it? Had his silence only deepened the rift? He didn't allow himself to linger on these thoughts for long. He couldn't afford to. There was too much at stake.

Work, too, was a challenge. The magazine world was less glamorous than he had imagined. His editor, Mr. Badhwar, was a hard man to please, dissecting each article with almost surgical precision. "Manohar, this is too rigid. I need heart, flair. Don't give me facts; give me life!" he had barked during one of their editorial meetings.

The newsroom itself was a battlefield of deadlines, politics, and unspoken rivalries. Manohar, still finding his footing, often felt like a novice among seasoned players who navigated the chaos with practised ease. They knew when to flatter, when to step aside, and when to push forward. Manohar's straightforwardness, while a virtue, sometimes left him adrift in the murky waters of office politics.

One evening, after yet another round of harsh feedback, Manohar sat in his cubicle, staring at the blinking cursor on his screen. His editor's words rang in his ears, challenging him to write not just with precision but with passion. The challenge wasn't merely professional—it was personal. Could he reconcile his journalistic duties with the expectations of his new role?

His ambition propelled him forward, even as it exacted a toll. Late nights at the office became routine, the glow of his computer screen his only companion. Meals were often skipped or replaced with hurried snacks grabbed on his way home. Exhaustion gnawed at him, but the fear of failure gnawed harder. Every article he submitted felt like a test of his worth, a measure of whether he belonged in this competitive world.

Calls from his family offered moments of warmth but also a heavy reminder of the expectations that followed him. "We're so proud of you, *beta*," his mother would say, her voice brimming with pride. Manohar would smile into the receiver, masking the weight of his struggles. Their dreams for him hung like an invisible thread, pulling him back to his roots even as he tried to move forward.

At night, the solitude of his flat magnified everything. The city outside seemed alive with stories, yet inside, his thoughts turned inward. He missed Simran in a way he hadn't expected, her words echoing in the quiet: "I love you forever." He didn't call her, didn't reach out. It wasn't indifference; it was fear—fear of complicating his already fragile equilibrium.

Noida's loneliness was different from the frantic isolation of Delhi. Here, in the quiet, he had time to think, to reflect. And with every passing day, he wrestled with the question that haunted him: had he made the right choice?

At work, his determination began to yield small victories. He learned to adapt and to write with more flair and emotion. His articles, once deemed too rigid, began to carry a touch of the heart his editor had demanded. But the deeper he delved into his work, the more distant he felt from everything else.

Simran's memory lingered, unshakeable. She surfaced in the oddest moments—during meetings, on his commute, and in the faces of strangers. He wondered if she was happy, if she had moved on. Part of him hoped she had, but another part—the part he buried deep—hoped she hadn't.

As days turned into weeks, Manohar settled into a rhythm. The initial excitement of independence faded, replaced by the grind of daily life. Yet, in the quiet of the night, when the city's lights dimmed, and the world slowed, the conflict within him surged to the surface. He had chosen duty over love, ambition over connection. But in the stillness, he couldn't help but wonder: was it worth it?

No matter how far he ran, the tug-of-war between his responsibilities and his heart never loosened its grip. In the quiet of his new beginnings, he learned a difficult truth: some conflicts don't resolve with time. They linger, waiting, until the moment comes when a choice must finally be made.

Chapter 32

CAREER PROGRESSION

The days after Manohar left for Noida were an emotional whirlwind for Simran. She would replay the moments of their last meeting—the tender exchange of sweets, the unspoken feelings that lingered in the air, and the bold confession that had escaped her lips. "I love you forever," she had said, her voice quivering with a mix of hope and vulnerability. Now, with his absence stretching before her like an endless horizon, a quiet ache settled in her chest.

In the beginning, Simran felt as though she had given away a piece of herself too soon, too openly. Doubts consumed her: Had she ruined everything between them? Would Manohar now see her differently? The fear of having overstepped haunted her, and the silence from his side only amplified her uncertainty.

But Simran wasn't one to stumble for long. There was a fire within her that refused to be extinguished. She realised that while Manohar had been a significant part of her journey, he was not the completeness of her story. Her life, her dreams and her ambitions were hers to chase, and she owed it to herself to keep moving forward.

One morning, as she stood before the mirror, Simran saw someone different staring back at her. Her reflection showed a woman determined to take charge of her life. She whispered to herself, "This is my time." That resolve sparked a change. She threw herself into her work at the institute with renewed energy, embracing every opportunity that came her way.

Simran's efforts didn't go unnoticed. Her mentors began assigning her more significant responsibilities, tasks that required leadership and vision. She thrived under this newfound trust, her confidence growing with every successful project. There was a deep satisfaction in knowing she was making a difference—shaping young minds, helping students navigate their paths, and being the guide she once wished she had.

Still, the nights were the hardest. After the bustle of the day faded, she would find herself alone in her room, the silence amplifying her thoughts. Memories of Manohar would resurface—the way he spoke, the gentle kindness in his eyes, the moments when it felt like he understood her without her having to say a word. Sometimes, she wondered if he missed her too or if his new life in Noida had already filled the space she once occupied in his heart.

But Simran was not the same person she had been when he left. The vulnerability of those first few days had transformed into a quiet strength. She was learning to stand tall, even in moments of doubt. Her work became her anchor, her solace, and she poured herself into it with unwavering focus.

Amidst this period of growth, Anjali returned to Simran's life like a breath of fresh air. Anjali, her childhood friend, had always been a source of light in her darkest moments. They had shared everything growing up—their dreams, their fears, and their hopes for the future. But in recent months, life had pulled them in different directions.

One evening, Anjali arrived unannounced, her arms open wide and her smile as bright as ever. "I've missed you, Simran," she said, enveloping her in a warm hug. They spent hours catching up, laughing over old memories and sharing stories about their current lives. But as the night deepened, Anjali gently steered the conversation towards the topic Simran had been avoiding.

"So," Anjali began, her voice soft but probing, "what's happening between you and your Sir?"

Simran hesitated, her fingers tracing the rim of her teacup. Finally, she sighed and said, "I don't know, Anjali. I miss him. I miss the way he made me feel—understood, and valued. But I also know I can't put my life on hold. I've been working on new projects and taking on challenges at the institute. It's fulfilling, but..." Her voice trailed off, and she looked away.

Anjali reached out, placing a comforting hand on Simran's. "But you still wonder if you made a mistake," she finished for her, her tone empathetic.

Simran nodded, her eyes glistening. "I wonder if I should have kept my feelings to myself, if saying those words pushed him away."

Anjali leaned forward, her expression firm yet compassionate. "Simran, being honest about your feelings isn't a mistake. It's brave. Love isn't something to regret or hide. You spoke your truth and that's all you could do. Now, it's up to him to figure out his path. But that doesn't mean you stop living yours."

Simran felt a lump rise in her throat but managed a faint smile. "You're right. I just... it's hard not knowing."

Anjali gave her a reassuring squeeze. "That's why you focus on what you can control. Your career, your goals, your happiness. You're talented and driven, Simran. Don't let the uncertainty hold you back. And who knows? Maybe in pursuing your own path, you'll find answers you never expected."

The words resonated deeply with Simran. She realised that waiting for clarity from someone else wasn't being fair to herself. Her journey was her own to define and whether or not Manohar would be part of her future, she needed to keep moving forward.

From that night onward, Simran embraced her career with even greater passion. She led workshops, mentored students, and even started a new initiative aimed at empowering young women to pursue their ambitions. Her work wasn't just a distraction—it was a testament to her resilience and her ability to rise above uncertainty.

And yet, in the quiet moments, when the world slowed down, a part of her heart still held space for Manohar. But now, that space was no longer a void; it was a reminder of her courage to love, to grow, and to keep moving forward. Simran was no longer defined by what she had lost but by everything she was becoming.

Simran smiled at her friend's words, letting a wave of comfort and reassurance wash over her. Anjali was right—she couldn't pause her life, waiting for someone else to make sense of theirs. Simran had her own dreams, her own ambitions, and it was time to give them the attention they deserved.

The weeks that followed marked the beginning of a quiet transformation. Determined to shape her future, Simran enrolled in a professional development course that promised to sharpen her skills and open new doors in her career. It wasn't an easy decision; the course demanded long hours of study and dedication. But Simran welcomed the challenge, diving into her studies with a passion she hadn't felt in a long time. Each lecture and each assignment felt like a small step towards reclaiming her independence and redefining her identity.

As the days turned into weeks, the pain of missing Manohar began to subside. It didn't vanish completely—there were still fleeting moments when his memory surfaced, uninvited. A familiar melody on the radio, a chance glimpse of someone with his posture, even a stray thought about what might have been—these could all bring him back to her mind. But the pangs of longing no longer consumed her. Slowly but surely, Simran found herself living more in the present and less in the shadow of the past.

She began to see herself through a new lens. Simran was no longer the young woman defined by unrequited love or the uncertainty of someone else's choices. She was a professional, a learner, a woman with dreams of her own. Her sense of purpose grew with every step forward, and she felt an unfamiliar but welcome pride in the person she was becoming.

The uncertainty of the future didn't frighten her anymore. She knew there would be challenges ahead, moments of doubt and vulnerability. But she also knew she had the strength to face them. Simran had discovered something profound in those weeks of change—not just who she could be without Manohar, but who she could be for herself.

Life wasn't perfect nor was it predictable. But it was hers to shape, and she was ready to embrace whatever came next. For the first time in a long time, Simran felt truly at peace—confident, capable and deeply proud of the woman she was becoming.

Chapter 33

UNEXPECTED ENCOUNTER

Months had passed since Simran and Manohar last exchanged words. Their lives had branched in different directions, like rivers flowing away from a shared source. Manohar, now firmly entrenched in his new job in Noida, had slipped into a routine of long workdays and solitary evenings. Simran, on the other hand, had poured herself into her career, determined to rise above the echo of her unreciprocated confession. Yet, no matter how far they had drifted, their memories gripped like the faint scent of a long-forgotten perfume.

The reunion came unexpectedly, as such things often do. A mutual friend's wedding brought together old acquaintances, a swirl of vibrant saris, cheerful banter, and celebratory music. Simran arrived with Anjali, dressed in a crimson sari that shimmered in the warm glow of the chandeliers. Confidence radiated from her like a soft beacon, drawing glances and smiles as she moved through the crowd.

It was as she laughed with a group of friends that her gaze fell on him. Manohar stood across the room, deep in conversation, his familiar posture and mannerisms pulling her back to the bittersweet moment when she'd last seen him. Her heart skipped a beat, then settled into a steady rhythm, not unlike the resolve she'd cultivated in recent months.

For a moment, Simran hesitated. She could turn away and avoid the encounter altogether. But the woman she had become wouldn't allow it. Straightening her shoulders, she took a deep breath and made her way towards him, her steps steady despite the racing of her heart.

Manohar noticed her before she reached him. His conversation faltered mid-sentence as his eyes locked onto hers. Time seemed to stretch, the room fading into a blur of colours and sound. She looked different—more poised, more self-assured. The shy girl he had once known had transformed into a woman who exuded a quiet strength.

"Simran," he said softly, his voice laced with surprise and something unspoken.

"Sir," she replied, her smile polite yet calm. "It's been a while."

The weight of their shared history hung in the air between them, a delicate thread that neither seemed ready to pull.

"You look... well," Manohar managed, his gaze lingering on her face.

"I am," Simran replied. "Life has been busy but good. I've been working on a few projects and taking a course. It's been fulfilling."

The confidence in her tone caught him off guard. This was not the Simran who had once been unsure of herself, who had looked to him for answers he hadn't been ready to give.

Manohar nodded, though his mind raced with memories and regrets. He had thought of her often during his quiet moments in Noida, her tearful confession replaying in his mind like an unsent letter. He had told himself that remaining silent was the right choice, a necessary one. Yet seeing her now, he wasn't so sure.

"You've changed," he said finally, his voice barely above a whisper.

Simran's smile deepened, though it carried a note of wistfulness. "I've grown. We both have."

For the first time, she addressed him by his first name. "Manohar, I don't want to dwell on the past. It was what it was. I've moved forward and I hope you have too."

Her words were simple, yet they carried the weight of her journey—a journey of self-discovery, independence and acceptance.

Their conversation drifted to safer topics—mutual friends, work, and the festivities around them. But the undercurrent of their unresolved history remained, a quiet murmur beneath the surface.

As the night wore on, Simran excused herself, the conversation concluding with a handshake and a soft smile. Manohar watched her walk away, his heart heavy with an unfamiliar mix of pride, admiration and perhaps regret.

For Simran, the encounter felt like closure, though not the kind she had once imagined. She had faced the man who had once held her heart and realised that her life was no longer defined by him. The twinge was still there, but it was a dull reminder of what she had overcome.

Both left the wedding that night with lingering thoughts of what had been—and what could still be. While their paths diverged once more, the quiet shift in their connection hinted at possibilities yet to unfold.

Chapter 34

FAMILY EXPECTATIONS

The oppressive heat of the summer day seemed to seep into every corner of Manohar's family home in Bihar. The buzz of a ceiling fan cut through the stillness, but it did little to dispel the tension that hung in the air. The living room bore the weight of countless family gatherings—a space where decisions about weddings, careers, and the future were debated, celebrated, and sometimes reluctantly accepted.

Seated on the faded cane chairs were Mr. and Mrs. Jha, their faces etched with both the wisdom of age and the unmistakable worry of parents with an unmarried son. Between them, on the low wooden table, sat a tray of untouched teacups and a small plate of sweets—symbolic offerings for a conversation that promised to be anything but sweet.

"Manohar," began his mother, her tone warm yet assertive, "it's time we discuss your future. You're not a boy anymore. You've started your career; now it's time to think about settling down."

Manohar shifted uncomfortably in his seat. He had known this moment was inevitable. In a household steeped in tradition, avoiding the subject of marriage was like trying to dodge the monsoon rains—it was only a matter of time before they caught up with you.

"I understand your concern, *Maa*," he began, his voice steady, though his hands betrayed his nerves by fidgeting with the hem of his kurta. "But right now, I need to focus on my job and building a solid foundation for myself."

Mrs. Jha sighed, her brow creasing. "You've been saying that for years. Meanwhile, your cousin Kumar is not only married but has a daughter! And what about your school friend Shashi? People are beginning to talk."

The dreaded "what will people say" argument. It was a phrase that carried the weight of societal expectations, one that had guided—and often dictated—the choices of countless families like his.

"Let them talk," Manohar replied, his voice firmer now. "I've always believed that marriage is about more than timing or convenience. I want to marry someone I truly connect with."

His father, who had been silent until now, finally spoke. "And do you think connections alone sustain a marriage? Respectability, shared values and a stable future are what matter. The girl we've found is from a reputed family we've known for years. They're interested, Manohar. Her father is eager to arrange a meeting."

Manohar's stomach sank. He could feel the walls of tradition closing in, even as his heart rebelled against it. He thought of Simran, the one person who had understood him without judgment. The memory of her confession lingered in his mind, a bittersweet reminder of what he might never have.

"Papa," he said carefully, choosing his words with precision, "I respect your judgement and the traditions of our family. But this is my life, and I need to be sure of what I want. I can't make such an important decision under pressure."

Mrs. Jha's expression softened, though her worry remained. She reached across the table to place a hand on his. "We're not pressuring you, *beta*. But marriage is a pillar of stability. We only want to see you happy and settled."

Manohar forced a smile, the weight of their expectations pressing down on him like the heat of the day. "I know you both mean well," he said quietly. "And I'll think about what you've said. But I'm asking for time—to figure out my path, to make sure that when I marry, it's the right decision for everyone involved."

The room fell silent, the only sound being the faint buzz of the fan overhead. His parents exchanged glances, their expressions a mixture of resignation and lingering hope.

As Manohar excused himself and stepped outside, the evening breeze offered little relief from the inner turmoil that churned within him. The familiar weight of family expectations bore down heavily on his shoulders and he wondered if he would ever find a way to balance his desires with the duty that tethered him to his roots.

For now, the path ahead remained uncertain, a delicate tightrope between tradition and the possibility of love.

Chapter 35

FAMILY TROUBLES

In Delhi, the oppressive heat of summer evenings often felt like a metaphor for the pressures simmering inside the Malhotra household. Simran sat at the dining table, her fingers idly tracing patterns on the wood. The scents of cumin and coriander wafted from the kitchen, where her mother, Mrs. Malhotra, stirred a pot of *dal* with the precision of someone who had been doing it her entire life.

Simran's thoughts, however, were far from the comforting aromas of home. They were tangled in a web of emotions she could barely articulate. Ever since her chance reunion with Manohar, her mind had been a whirlpool of memories, questions and unspoken longings.

"Simran, dear, are you even listening to me?" Mrs. Malhotra's voice sliced through her reverie like a sharp knife.

Startled, Simran glanced up. "Yes, Mum. What were you saying?"

Mrs. Malhotra sighed, her hands busy wiping flour from her saree. "I was talking about the Sharma family down the street. Their son is such a nice boy—polite, well-employed and from a good family. They're looking for a match for him, and I thought, maybe..."

The words hung in the air, unfinished but unmistakable. Simran's chest tightened and her appetite vanished entirely.

"Mum," she interrupted, her voice taut, "I'm not ready to think about marriage right now."

Her mother turned from the gas stove, eyebrows arched in mild disapproval. "Not ready? Simran, you're not getting any younger. What's there to wait for? You can't just let the right opportunities pass you by. Your father and I only want the best for you."

"Best for me?" Simran echoed, her frustration bubbling dangerously close to the surface. "And what about what I want? You think I can just marry someone because the timing feels convenient? What if I don't feel anything for him?"

Mrs. Malhotra paused, her expression softening, though her resolve remained firm. "Love, *beta*, isn't always about fireworks and grand gestures. It's about building a life together. Feelings grow with time. What matters more are the practicalities—a good family and a stable life. Isn't that what truly counts?"

Simran's throat tightened. Her mother's words, though well-meaning, felt like a dismissal of everything she believed in. "Mom," she said softly, tears welling in her eyes, "I already have feelings for someone."

A silence fell over the room, broken only by the faint hiss of the stove. Mrs. Malhotra turned to face her daughter fully, her expression now one of curiosity tinged with concern. "Someone? Who is it, Simran? Is it someone we know?"

Simran hesitated, the weight of the moment pressing down on her. "It's Sir... Manohar," she admitted, her voice barely above a whisper. "But he's in Noida now, and I don't even know if he feels the same way."

The name landed heavily between them. Mrs. Malhotra's face stiffened, her brows knitting together in a mixture of shock and worry. "Manohar?" she repeated slowly. "He's... not from our community, is he? Simran, you know how your father feels about these things. This isn't just about you. It's about the family, our values, and our reputation."

Simran felt her chest tighten further. "Why does it always have to be about caste and community?" she asked, her voice trembling. "Why can't love be enough? Why do I have to give up my happiness for the sake of traditions I never chose?"

Mrs. Malhotra stepped closer, her tone gentler now, though no less resolute. "Sweetheart, I understand how you feel. But society doesn't change overnight. These traditions aren't just rules—they're the foundation of how we live. They protect us and give us structure. It's not just about love; it's about building a life that fits into the world we live in."

Simran turned away, her vision blurred with unshed tears. She felt like a bird trapped in a cage, her wings clipped by expectations she had no desire to meet.

The night wore on, and dinner was served in uneasy silence. Simran barely touched her food, her mind replaying her mother's words alongside the memory of Manohar's face. Somewhere, she knew her mother's concerns came from love, but the bitterness of her own unfulfilled dreams was impossible to ignore.

Across the city, as Manohar wrestled with his parents' expectations, Simran found herself similarly entangled. The love that had once felt so simple and pure was now shrouded in complexities neither of them knew how to navigate.

As darkness settled over Delhi, two hearts beat in quiet turmoil, each yearning for the other yet weighed down by forces beyond their control. The distance between them wasn't just physical—it was a gap carved by tradition, duty and the unrelenting demands of family. And as they lay awake in their respective homes, the same question haunted them both: how much of themselves were they willing to sacrifice for love?

Chapter 36

LOVE VS TRADITION

Manohar sat hunched over his jumbled desk in the magazine office, the warm afternoon sun slicing through the blinds and pooling across the papers scattered before him. Outside his window, life carried on with its usual rhythm, but inside, Manohar felt caught in a storm of indecision. The chatter and clatter of keyboards from his colleagues felt distant, muffled beneath the weight of his thoughts.

Since his move to Noida, his days had been a whirlwind of deadlines and articles, yet the memory of Simran lingered, vivid and persistent. Her tear-filled confession was etched into his mind, replaying in quiet moments like a bittersweet melody he couldn't escape. But reality loomed large—his family's expectations, their insistence on tradition and the inevitability of an arranged marriage. The happiness he yearned for felt like a flickering light, tantalizingly out of reach.

"Manohar!"

The voice jolted him from his reverie. It was Rajesh, a senior colleague who had taken on the role of mentor since Manohar's first day at the magazine. With his salt-and-pepper hair and an appearance shaped by years of newsroom chaos, Rajesh exuded a quiet authority.

"You've been staring at that same sheet of paper for half an hour," Rajesh said, leaning against the edge of Manohar's desk. "Care to share what's occupying that restless mind of yours?"

Manohar hesitated, his fingers tracing the edge of a notebook. Finally, he sighed, his words spilling out like a confession. "It's my family... They want me to marry someone they've chosen. But there's someone else—someone I can't stop thinking about."

Rajesh tilted his head thoughtfully, his eyes narrowing as he listened. "Love, huh? That's a slippery slope, my friend. It's beautiful but often messy. The real question is, what do you want?"

"I think about it every day," Manohar admitted, his voice barely audible. "Simran confessed her feelings to me before I left Delhi. I care about her—deeply. But my parents have already started talking about this other girl. They say she's perfect, someone who aligns with our family's traditions. I feel trapped."

Rajesh crossed his arms, his tone shifting to one of quiet intensity. "Let me tell you something, Manohar. Family and tradition—they're important, yes. But you can't live your life as a shadow of their expectations. Picture yourself ten years from now. If you make a choice that isn't yours, will you be able to look in the mirror without regret?"

The question struck a chord. Manohar leaned back in his chair, staring at the ceiling as Rajesh's words sank in. "But what about the consequences? If I go against their wishes, it could break their hearts. And what will people say? The community... they'll judge us, maybe even ostracise us."

"Let them talk," Rajesh said, his voice resolute. "Tradition isn't a set of chains, Manohar—it's a compass. It points the way, but you don't have to follow it blindly. Talk to your parents. Be honest about what you want. You might be surprised by their response."

That evening, back in his modest apartment, Manohar found himself lying in bed, staring at the ceiling fan as it hummed softly overhead. The room was dim, illuminated only by the faint glow of streetlights filtering through the curtains. His mind drifted to Simran—her earnest gaze, her trembling voice as she had confessed, "Sir, I love you forever."

He thought about the moments they had shared—their laughter, the conversations that stretched long into the evenings, and the dreams they had hesitantly spoken of, as though afraid the world would snatch them away.

Could he really give all of that up for a life dictated by duty? Or did he owe it to himself—and to Simran—to fight for what they shared?

Manohar's chest tightened as he imagined the confrontation with his parents. He could already hear their voices, their disappointment palpable. But Rajesh's words lingered in his mind: Tradition isn't a prison.

As the hours crept by, Manohar felt a clarity begin to emerge. The road ahead was fraught with uncertainty, but he knew one thing for sure: he couldn't ignore his heart. Tomorrow, he would make a call—not to Simran, not yet—but to his parents. The time had come to face his fears and take the first step towards a future he could call his own.

In the quiet of the night, with the city's buzz as his backdrop, Manohar made his decision. It wasn't just about love or tradition anymore—it was about reclaiming his life, no matter how daunting the journey ahead might seem.

Chapter 37

AT A CROSSROADS

Simran paced her small bedroom, the dim light casting shadows that seemed to mirror her inner turmoil. Her mind replayed the last conversation with Manohar, each word carving deeper grooves of uncertainty. She had exposed her heart and laid her emotions bare, only to be met with responses that left her grappling with more questions than answers.

Days blurred into weeks, and the silence between them grew deafening. It was as though an invisible chasm had opened, widening with every passing moment. To cope, Simran buried herself in work, pouring all her energy into her career. But no amount of professional success could fill the void in her heart. She was trapped—waiting for a love that might never materialise.

Late one evening, as rain softly pattered against her window, her best friend Anjali visited for a casual coffee chat. The familiar aroma of their late-night brews failed to mask the tension.

"You've changed, Simran," Anjali said, her eyes narrowing with concern. "You're always somewhere else— lost in thought. What's going on with you and Manohar?"

Simran sighed deeply, her shoulders slumping under the weight of her secret. "I told him I love him, Anjali. I opened my heart, but now... I don't even know where we stand. I can't keep waiting like this. I have dreams and ambitions, but my heart keeps pulling me back to him."

Anjali tilted her head, her expression softening. "You deserve to be happy, Simran. Maybe it's time to think about moving on. What if there's someone else out there who can love you the way you deserve?"

Simran shook her head, her voice barely a whisper. "My heart belongs to him. But what if he never comes back? What if I'm holding on to something that's never meant to be?"

As if on cue, a new figure entered her life: Rohan, a charismatic colleague who seemed genuinely intrigued by her. He admired her work and often found excuses to linger by her desk, inviting her to coffee or lunch. Simran appreciated his kindness, yet every glance at him reminded her of Manohar. Was it fair to explore something new while her heart still clung to a love that felt so unfinished?

Weeks passed, and Simran found herself at a crossroads. Rohan's persistence was undeniable—he was gentle, attentive and understanding. Yet, even in his presence, her thoughts drifted back to Manohar. The choice loomed over her like a storm cloud: should she open her heart to Rohan or hold onto the fragile hope that Manohar might return her love?

A FINAL GOODBYE

One evening, as thunder roared faintly in the distance, Simran made a decision. She couldn't bear the uncertainty any longer. She had to confront Manohar—lay everything on the line and demand clarity. Her fingers trembled as she dialled his number.

"Hello?" His voice, deep and familiar, sent a pang through her chest.

"Manohar," she began, her voice steadier than she felt, "can we meet? There's something I need to say."

"Of course, Simran. Where should we meet?"

"Bonta Park," she said, the words tumbling out before she could reconsider. "You remember... the place we used to go?"

The park, once a sanctuary of laughter and whispered promises, now felt like a distant memory. The air was thick with unspoken words as Simran and Manohar stood at the crossroads of their lives. They had shared so much— the dreams, the moments of joy, the quiet understanding between them. But now, that bond seemed fragile, as if it might crumble at the slightest touch. The ground beneath their feet felt uncertain, the path ahead unclear.

As they walked side by side, the silence between them grew heavier with each step. Simran's heart ached with a mixture of love and longing. She had imagined a future where they were together, where they could overcome every obstacle, where love would be enough. But now, standing at the edge of this moment, she wondered if she had been wrong all along.

"I thought we would find a way to make this work," Simran finally said, her voice barely above a whisper, the words slipping out before she could stop them. "But I understand if you can't."

Manohar turned to her, his expression torn, as though he too were battling the same storm inside. "Simran, I wish things were different. I really do. I wish I could fight for us without the weight of my family's expectations bearing down on me. But I can't keep you waiting. You deserve to be happy."

Tears glistened in Simran's eyes, and she fought to keep them at bay. "I don't want to say goodbye," she said, her voice breaking. "But I also don't want to hold you back. You have to live your life, Manohar."

Manohar nodded, his own heart heavy with the burden of his choices. "You're right. I can't let my family's traditions dictate my happiness. But at the same time, I can't deny the love and respect I have for them. It's a conflict I can't resolve just yet."

Simran stepped back, feeling the emotional distance between them growing by the second. "So what now?" she asked, her voice trembling.

"Now," Manohar said, his voice tinged with sorrow, "we must part ways. But that doesn't mean we have to forget what we shared."

The words hung in the air, a quiet promise that neither of them could break. They stood there for a long moment, hands not quite reaching for each other, their hearts still tangled in a love that had once been so certain but now felt like a dream slipping away.

Manohar took a deep breath, his look intense, as if trying to hold on to something that was slipping through his fingers. "You will always hold a special place in my heart, Simran," he said, his voice full of conviction. "I want you to pursue your dreams, to find happiness—even if it's not with me."

Simran managed a small smile, though it didn't reach her eyes. His words were a balm to her aching heart, but they also reminded her of everything they were losing. "And you, Manohar," she replied, her voice steady but soft. "Follow your path, whatever that may be. I hope you find the happiness you deserve."

With those final words, Simran reached out and took his hand, her touch remaining for just a moment longer than necessary. "Thank you," she said quietly. "Thank you for everything—the memories, the love. I will always cherish them."

The moment felt suspended in time as if the world around them had faded into the background. And then, with a final glance at each other, they stepped back, the distance between them suddenly insurmountable. The park, once filled with laughter, now seemed eerily quiet, the air heavy with the weight of their decisions. They turned to walk away, each step a reminder of the love they had lost and the lives they were about to begin forever.

That June 8th had been the hardest, which etched itself into his memory. It was a day of significance—a day that seemed destined to mark turning points in his life.

Chapter 39

MOVING ON

The months that followed the difficult decision weighed heavily on Simran's heart. Yet, in the face of the pain, she found a surprising solace in her work. She threw herself into her career, channelling her sadness into something productive. The weight of her emotions, once overwhelming, became a driving force behind her ambition. She enrolled in advanced counselling courses, determined to perfect her skills and prove that her worth was not tied to her past or her heart's desires.

Her commitment soon bore fruit. Word of her expertise spread, and recognition followed. People began to seek her guidance, and her reputation grew within her profession. It wasn't the life she had once dreamed of, but it was a life she could hold onto. Slowly, the throbbing in her chest began to soften, transforming from sorrow into a quiet strength. As she helped others navigate their emotional struggles, she found healing for her own.

Then, as if life had a way of bringing unexpected gifts, Simran met Munna. He was different—a man who not only understood her need for independence but also celebrated it. He supported her dreams, never imposing expectations on her, but standing beside her as a partner in every sense. Their relationship blossomed naturally, built on mutual respect, understanding and shared values. When they married in an intimate intercaste ceremony, it wasn't just a union of two people. It was a victory—a celebration of love defying societal barriers, of their commitment to each other and the start of a new chapter for Simran.

Far away, Manohar returned to his hometown. The expectations were high, and the pressure to settle down weighed heavily on him. His family, eager to see him married, made their desires clear, and after much contemplation, Manohar reluctantly agreed to the match his parents had arranged.

June 8th arrived, carrying with it the quiet promise of a fresh beginning. It was a date that had once symbolised the weight of unfulfilled dreams, but now, it marked the start of a new chapter in his life. It was a date that would forever be etched in his memory, but now it marked the beginning of a different chapter in his life. He wasn't at a crossroads anymore; this was a new start, though not without its echoes of the past.

Neetu, his bride, was everything Manohar needed: practical, grounded, and deeply respectful of the values that had been instilled in him. She understood him in ways that Simran never had, and while the memories of Simran would forever be a part of his heart, Manohar chose to embrace the life that had been laid out for him. On his wedding day, standing beside Neetu, he felt a sense of peace—peace that came not from the romantic ideal he had once dreamed of but from the quiet acceptance of his reality.

As the ceremony continued, with laughter and music filling the air, Manohar found a moment of solitude. He glanced towards the horizon, a silent prayer escaping his lips for Simran. He wished for her happiness, for the peace he hoped she had found in her choices.

In time, Manohar adjusted to his new life, learning that love can take many forms. It wasn't the passionate, all-consuming love he had once imagined with Simran, but it was love nonetheless—steady and grounded, with a sense of comfort and companionship that he hadn't realised he'd been missing.

✳ ✳ ✳

And so, time passed. Simran and Manohar continued their separate journeys, each finding their own way forward, each carving out a new version of happiness. Their shared moments from the past no longer felt like a weight they had to carry. Instead, they were memories—beautiful, bittersweet and ever-present—but no longer burdens.

Simran thrived in her career, becoming not just a counsellor, but an inspiration of hope and guidance for those who needed her. Her marriage to Munna, too, flourished. They built their life together on a foundation of love, respect and shared dreams. In him, Simran found a partner who cherished her not for who she had been with Manohar, but for who she was becoming.

Manohar, in turn, found happiness in his life with Neetu. The love he carried for Simran would always be a part of him, but he had learned to appreciate the stability and companionship he had found with her. Life, as he now understood, was not always about the kind of love that swept you off your feet; sometimes, it was about the steady love that rooted you, the kind that grew stronger with time, built on trust and understanding.

As the years went by, both Simran and Manohar knew that love doesn't always mean staying together. Sometimes, it's about moving on. It's about choosing the paths that lead to growth, happiness and independence. They had let go, not because they didn't love each other, but because love, in its truest form, is often about letting go and giving each other the freedom to grow.

And so, as the sun set on their past, Simran and Manohar faced the future with hope in their hearts. Their paths had diverged, but their spirits remained strong, their hearts full of dreams and their courage unshaken. The question remained in their minds: What lies ahead for those brave enough to embrace change and trust in the love they've built, even if it's not the love they once expected?

Chapter 40

AFTER 35 YEARS

Thirty-five years had passed since Manohar Kumar had walked the winding roads of youth and now, as he sat quietly in his home in Noida, the weight of those years felt both distant and profound. Life had unfolded in ways he hadn't quite imagined, and yet, the family he had built, with his wife Neetu at its heart, was his anchor in a world that seemed to change with every breath.

The house, now a mix of tradition and modernity, thrived with the energy of three generations. His octogenarian parents, once vibrant pillars of the home, now required more care, and their presence was both a gentle reminder of time's passage and a source of unwavering comfort. His children, though grown and walking their own paths, remained the threads weaving together his past and present.

His son, a confident young man with a B.Tech degree, had found his place in the corporate world. His daughter, however, was the true reflection of a dream fulfilled. Following in his footsteps, she entered the competitive world of words, landing a coveted role in a national media house. Every article she penned, every by-line she earned, filled Manohar with immense pride. Through her, he felt as though his unfulfilled aspirations had been realised.

But it was at the dinner table, where the moments of daily life met the deeper currents of thought that Manohar's mind often wandered. One evening, his son asked a question that shook him to his core.

"Papa," his son began, "why was your generation so bound by caste? Why didn't love and individuality matter more?"

Manohar's eyes grew distant for a moment, the weight of the past settling heavily on his chest. "We carried the burden of expectations, son," he said, his voice quiet but firm. "Tradition was our guide, even when it led us down paths we didn't choose. It was never simple and it was never easy."

His son, with all the confidence of youth, often challenged the very principles that had shaped Manohar's world. He was a child of the modern age, where the ideals of caste and tradition seemed outdated. In his son's eyes, Manohar saw a reflection of all the changes he had hoped for, yet was unable to fully embrace. It was a bittersweet hope that his son would make the choices he had never been brave enough to make. It's quite astonishing—despite growing up in the heart of Delhi, where love stories blossom faster than metro lines, his son and daughter never fell into the usual love mate entanglements.

Neetu, his wife, remained the silent strength of their home. She balanced the duties of motherhood and wife with grace, tending to the needs of both their children and his ageing parents. Yet, her sacrifices, often unseen by the world, were not without their own cost.

"Why do you take on so much?" her friends would ask, their words casual but laced with judgment. "Let the younger generation take care of things."

Their comments stung, leaving a quiet ache in Neetu's heart. One evening, as they sat together after the children had gone to bed, she voiced her doubts to Manohar.

"Am I wrong to care so much?" she asked, her voice barely above a whisper. "Sometimes it feels like no one values these bonds anymore."

Manohar, ever the anchor, reached for her hand, his touch gentle but sure. "Neetu," he said softly, "the strength of a family is built on love. You are the cornerstone of ours. Not everyone will understand that, but it doesn't change what you've created."

Despite the occasional doubts that lingered in her heart, Neetu continued, her resilience unshaken. For her, love was not just an emotion but a force that bound their family together, one unspoken bond at a time.

As for Simran, the woman who had once held his heart in a tender, delicate grip, time had carried her far from the days when their futures had seemed intertwined. She was happily married, raising a son of her own, and though their paths had parted, their connection, grounded in shared memories, remained. Their occasional reunions were quiet celebrations of what had been and what could never be—a friendship built not on what was lost but on the understanding of what was once shared.

Amit and Prita's lives had taken a different shape entirely. Prita, having embraced spirituality, had chosen a life of solitude and reflection, while Amit, with quiet dedication, continued to raise their daughters. Their unconventional arrangement spoke of a peace found in acceptance and the beauty of carving your own path, however unconventional it might be.

Now, as Manohar sat on the veranda, reflecting on his life, the thought of all the unspoken bonds he had carried, and the ones that had shaped him, filled his mind. These were not bonds defined by words but by actions, sacrifices and silent understandings. The connection with Simran, the unshakeable support of Neetu and the shared values passed down to his children—these were the threads that held his story together.

But it was his son who lingered in Manohar's thoughts. Standing on the edge of decisions that would shape his future, the question remained: would he, too, be bound by the traditions that had once held his father captive? Would he dare to choose love over convention?

Now that Manohar's son has reached marriageable age, a steady stream of proposals comes his way. Families from their community, drawn to his sharp intellect and striking appearance, eagerly express their interest. Manohar watches the flurry of discussions with quiet amusement, half expecting his son to push back against the weight of expectations—just as he once had.

But what truly catches him off guard is his son's unwavering stance. After years of observing his father's choices, listening to unspoken regrets, and absorbing the silent lessons of a lifetime, he has made up his mind. He wants to marry within his own caste, to uphold the traditions he has grown up with. His voice carries no doubt, no hesitation.

For a moment, Manohar feels something tighten in his chest. He had spent years questioning these very customs, struggling between love and duty, and yet, here is his son—embracing them without a second thought. He wonders if his own battles had left any imprint at all. Had his son ever glimpsed the unspoken pain beneath his carefully composed face? Or had he, unknowingly, passed down the very ideals he once longed to escape?

The realization stings. Life, it seems, has a way of circling back in unexpected ways, rewriting old struggles into new chapters—ones he never imagined reading.

As the sun dipped below the horizon, casting a golden hue over the world, Manohar closed his magazine and sat back in his chair, a quiet smile forming on his lips. Life, he realised, was not about the choices made but about the courage to live through them. The road may not have been straight, nor the decisions easy, but it had been rich with love, growth and the lessons of time.

At that moment, as he looked out into the fading light, a thought rooted itself in his heart: The crossroads of the heart—between love, duty, and choice—are not meant to